Pictures in the Cave

George Mackay Brown lives and works in the Orkney Islands where he was born. He went to Newbattle Abbey College in Midlothian and later read English at Edinburgh University. He has never travelled further south than Scotland.

Amongst the awards he has received as a writer are the Scottish Arts Council Literature Prize in 1969, the Katherine Mansfield Short Story Prize in 1971 and the OBE in 1974. *Pictures in the Cave* is his second book for young people.

Also by
George Mackay Brown in Piccolo
The Two Fiddlers

George Mackay Brown

Pictures in the Cave

text illustrations by Ian MacInnes
cover illustration by Paul Slater

Scholastic in association with Pan Books

First published 1977 by Chatto & Windus Ltd
This edition published for Scholastic Publications Ltd,
161 Fulham Road, London SW3 6SW by
Pan Books Ltd, Cavaye Place, London SW10 9PG
© George Mackay Brown 1977
illustrations © Ian MacInnes 1977
ISBN 0 330 25773 0
Set, printed and bound in Great Britain by
Cox & Wyman Ltd, Reading

to Fiona and Mhairi

Contents

The truant

Sigurd woke, as every morning, with sea noises in his ear. He drowsed awhile in his bed, and turned over, and half sank into sleep again ... He was woken with a vengeance by din and clangour from the smithy at the end of the house! His father Ron Bressay's work day had begun.

There could be no sleep after that. Besides, his mother sent the first of her summonses upstairs, 'Boy, your breakfast's on the table!' Two minutes later the urgent voice came again. 'Sigurd, you'll be late for school! Willie Tarbreck's just gone up the road.'

Sigurd put on desolation with his shirt and trousers. He had not greatly cared for the school on the hillside since his first day there. Still, he went because it was the thing to do –

all the island children had to attend school till they were fourteen at least. There were some things about school, in truth, that Sigurd enjoyed: stories, and poems, and history, and geography. And old Miss Walterson had been a kind teacher. On fine summer days she let them out to gather flowers and shells; these delightful periods were called 'nature study'. Every Friday afternoon she passed round the school a big rustling bag of sweets. At the end of every term the pupils were given a new bright penny each.

But last summer Miss Walterson had retired and a new schoolmaster was appointed, Mr Prosser. Mr Prosser was a different kettle of fish. He was strict, for one thing. The island children were appalled at the way Mr Prosser shouted sometimes – they had never heard such thunders out of any man's mouth. The lips of some of them would tremble when Mr Prosser raised his voice – even, sometimes, if he chanced to look rather stern.

Sometimes a demon entered into Mr Prosser and he would lash out right and left with the 'strap' he kept on his desk. It lay coiled there most of the time like a sleeping snake. The strap was a length of thick leather split into a forked tongue at one end. When Mr Prosser wielded it the venom and rage fell on the open outstretched palm of the culprit's hand. If you were late for school you would be 'strapped'. If you made some awful mistake in arithmetic; if you whispered to your class neighbour; if you spilled ink on the floor; if you were caught exchanging cigarette cards under the desk; if some sneak like Willie Tarbreck reported you for saying 'a bad-word' in the playground; above all if you hadn't done your homework, the coiled snake was aroused from its desk-sleep. The old islanders had a good name for this ancient instrument of punishment – they called it the 'tawse'.

Sigurd reflected miserably, as he went downstairs, that on

two counts he would get the tawse that day. First, he would certainly be late. He could see through the open door Ollie Rolfson running along the road schoolwards, and Ollie was *always* late. Second, he hadn't done his homework.

His breakfast was ready on the table: boiled egg and buttered scone, and cup of milk.

His school-bag lay on the chair next the door, with the neglected books inside.

There was a basin of lukewarm water on the stand in the corner for him to wash his face and hands in.

The sun set its blazon on the doorstep.

His mother was out, seeing to the sickly lamb he supposed. Sigurd decided to forgo washing and eating. He seized the school-bag and ran out into the sunshine before his mother could come and begin again her kindly hectoring.

There his mother was indeed, at the end of the field, bent over the tottery lamb with a feeding-bottle in her hand. Sigurd slipped past the open door of the smithy. His father was a black strenuous silhouette against the glare of the forge. He went on. He suddenly realized that he was walking not towards the school but towards the high western end of the island with its cliffs and wheeling birds and tumults of sea.

As he walked on Sigurd was possessed with a sense of wild freedom such as he only felt on the first day of the summer holiday, when an eternity seven weeks long opened up before him. He laughed. He began to run and caper along the grass verge.

'I am a wicked bad useless boy,' Sigurd proclaimed to the blackbird in Minnie Pow's bush. 'I am playing truant from school. I am not sick at all – I have just decided not to go. I will be in serious trouble. Mr Prosser will thrash me within an inch of my life.'

The blackbird chortled out of the bush. It seemed to be hugely enjoying Sigurd's confession.

'I'll tell you something too,' said Sigurd. 'I haven't done my homework.'

The blackbird danced and throbbed in the bush with joy.

Sigurd sat down in a ditch teeming with buttercups. 'Let's have a look,' he said, 'at this homework I was supposed to do. It was poetry.' . . . The blackbird was making its own sonnets and odes. Minnie Pow's garden was a marvellous anthology.

Sigurd had liked poetry well enough in Miss Walterson's time. But Mr Prosser dealt out poetry by the pound and the yard, as if he was trading in some kind of distasteful merchandise. 'You will all learn the following piece of verse by heart and be word-perfect tomorrow morning. Page 134 in your poetry books. Otherwise there'll be trouble.' . . . That's what Mr Prosser had said yesterday afternoon last thing.

Idly Sigurd opened the book – two white halves in the sunlight – at page 134:

Come, dear children, let us away:
   Down and away below!
Now my brothers call the bay;
   Now the great winds shoreward blow;
   Now the salt tides seaward flow;
Now the wild white horses play,
Champ and chafe and toss in the spray,
Children dear, let us away!
   This way, this way!

Sigurd liked that very much – the sound and the rhythms and an old mysterious sea-pain. 'O yes,' he said. 'But think what Prosser will do with it. He will make it into an instrument of torture for young children . . . Gosh, I'm hungry.'

Just then Sigurd heard an old wise voice coming from the garden wall. 'Well, well. Well, well. What's this? What's this? Not at the school, not at the school. Have you been sent home for being bad? Who are you, boy? Who are you?'... Minnie Pow said nearly everything twice.

Sigurd got to his feet.

'The boy from the Smithy – the Smithy boy. Would you like something to drink – a cup of something good to drink. Come in, come in, Smithy boy.'

But Sigurd refused to go in, quite politely. He had chosen to spend the day out of doors. He had no intention of sitting all morning in an old cat-and-hen-and-peat smelling parlour. 'Please,' he said, 'I'll drink it outside.'

Muttering about truants and tawses the old one disappeared into her cottage. She came back and put a bottle in Sigurd's hand. (He had been expecting a cup of milk.)

'Where are you going now, boy? Where?'

Sigurd said he thought he might go down to the Bay of Seals. It stretched for a mile, all rock and sand and thunders of sea, just a hundred yards down from Minnie's door.

'Don't go near the cave,' said Minnie Pow darkly. 'Never the cave. Keep well clear of that cave.'

Sigurd knew all about the cave. A witch had lived in it hundreds of years ago – a terrible witch called Jenny who stewed children in a pot and drank their blood. The black enchantment still lingered about the cave. Only the bravest of the island children would venture more than a few yards into that dreadful orifice. The cave kept its old spells.

'I'll take care,' said Sigurd. 'Thank you for the bottle of lemonade.'

'Cheerio,' said the blackbird. 'Well done, boy. Cheerio.'

As he exchanged the dusty road for sand and rockpool and horizon, Sigurd could hear a remote tinkle. The school was being summoned back from the play interval ... The poetry-torture would begin in a few minutes.

Sigurd laughed. He wandered slowly along the beach,

leaving an erratic trail of footprints. (He had put his sandals into the school-bag, beside bottle and poetry book.)

Two ships sailed along the western horizon, going between Europe and America. A pang of longing went through the boy, for far quests and boundless freedom. He thought he might like to be a sailor when he grew up.

He sat down on a flat rock quite near the cave-mouth. Out on the skerry that ran into the sea like a ragged sword a cluster of seals were basking in the light. One swam free, his head bobbing sleek in the fast-flowing hushing crisping murmurous Sound. 'A wicked worthless boy,' said Sigurd to himself, mimicking the voices of authority in the island: minister, teacher, Mr Tarbreck the county councillor ... 'Imagine it, a boy who'd rather sit outside a witch-cave than in a fine school where he'll learn to make progress, get on in the world, and improve himself!' ... 'A good-for-nothing, a waster, a drinker in the noon-day sun!'

Sigurd smiled and took the bottle out of his school-bag. When he opened it it gave a surprised 'pop', then the liquor inside lapsed into murmurs and whispers rather like shell-music when you hold one of those cold intricate sea-shapes to the shell of your ear. But this was the dark song of the earth. Sigurd sniffed – it wasn't lemonade at all, it was ale, a very famous brew. 'Minnie's ale,' the old men would say approvingly in the smithy on a winter evening, and nod and smile. 'Minnie's ale is a very good ale.'

Sigurd's stomach was so empty – he hadn't eaten since tea-time last night – that he drained the bottle in six or seven deep gulps. At once the world seemed to break apart and then rearrange itself on a pattern nearer to his heart's desire; he was certain that no such place as the school existed; this new world belonged to seals, witches, truants, sailors! 'All the same,' he hiccuped, 'Jenny oughtn't to have made stew out of boys and girls.'

'Jenny did no such thing. Jenny was good,' said a voice.

Who had spoken? Sigurd paused and looked in every direction. There was not a living creature to be seen, except the head of the young seal that broke the sea surface a cable-length out.

'Jenny put curses on beast and field,' Sigurd said. 'She made spells and killed people. What a wrinkled ugly old thing she must have been!'

'Oh no, she wasn't! Jenny was the sweetest lass that ever lived in this island.' ...

The voice came again after a pause. 'Come into the sea, boy. I'll tell you the story of Jenny. I know all about her. She was my great-great-great-great-great-great grandmother.'

There was no doubt about it. The voice belonged to the seal.

'That cave,' said the seal, and its voice sounded sweet and cold across the water, 'there's nothing to be afraid of in that cave, boy. More wonderful things have happened in that cave than in any house in the island, including the Hall and the Manse. You wouldn't believe all the things that have happened. I don't suppose there's ever been such a beautiful girl in this island as Jenny Stoor.'

'An old witch,' said Sigurd, repeating what he had been told over and over again at the croft fires in winter. 'She drank children's blood.'

'Do you want to hear about Jenny?' said the seal. 'Do you want to know the whole history of the cave? Or do you want to go on repeating nonsense like a parrot till you're a tiresome old man?'

'I like the truth,' said Sigurd, 'so long as it's interesting.'

'Come into the sea then,' said the seal. 'When stories are told in the sea a magic gets into them. You can swim beside me, I'll tell you all about Jenny.'

'I won't,' said Sigurd. 'No fear.'

The seal had all the time been coming closer inshore. Now Sigurd could see his large beautiful liquid eyes and his fine whiskers.

'Sigurd,' said the seal. 'I've taken a fancy to you. Are you surprised that I know your name? The seals know everything about the island and the islanders. We seals have been taking note of you for the past summer or two. "Sigurd," we say to each other, "he's a good boy, he doesn't throw stones and sticks and bottles at us, like that Willie Tarbreck." ... Sometimes we say, "Sigurd now, he's a friend of the seals. Some time we must share some of our secrets with him. Not all of them, for he wouldn't understand. But we could tell him what a wonderful place the cave is, really. Sigurd belongs to the sea more than to the land. Some day, when Sigurd's in trouble, we'll do something for him." ' ...

'I never knew that seals could speak,' said Sigurd.

'Some of them can,' said the seal. 'Those of us who've had island men or island girls among our ancestors. They can sing and dance and eat chocolate as well as you can.'

By this time the seal was half ashore. It lay on the sand not six yards away from Sigurd.

'So, Sigurd,' said the seal, 'if you won't come to us, into the water, I'll have to come and be your friend on the land.'

You know how clumsy seals are on skerry or shore. They flounder about awkwardly, they blunder slowly and inefficiently here and there. On land they have none of the sweet fluent powerful grace with which they move in the sea after trout or haddocks.

Sigurd thought to himself, 'He's a good seal. I like him. How wonderful, that the seals have been speaking nicely about me! I'm eager to hear what he has to say. But I suppose it'll take him a good ten minutes to blunder up the beach to where I am.' . . . And he thought, to save the seal all that trouble, that he would walk down to the water's edge to meet him.

Then an astonishing thing happened. As soon as the seal was clear of the water, it reared up and its skin slipped down to the sand. What had been a seal was a white-skinned boy. Sigurd had never seen such an enchanting face and such a lissom beautiful body. The seal-boy approached, smiling. At last he stood beside Sigurd, with his sealskin hanging over one shoulder. They laid wondering hands together, and smiled shyly, face into face, for a long time.

'Tell me your name,' said Sigurd.

'You wouldn't be able to pronounce it,' said the seal-boy. 'It's full of sea-sounds, like the wave on the rock out there, or the whisperings of the seaweed in the turning tide, and it has silence too in it like the stillness after a storm . . . You can call me Shelmark if you like.'

'Hello, Shelmark,' said Sigurd.

'Sigurd,' said Shelmark, 'I promised to tell you the truth about Jenny. I think we should sit down on this rock side by side. The story takes some time to tell.'

'What if the school attendance officer comes looking for me?' said Sigurd.

'It doesn't matter,' said Shelmark. 'Don't worry about him. Tam of Smelt is such a coarse-grained creature he wouldn't see me. Mr Prosser isn't that much better.'

They sat on the rock, the boy in the grey patched jersey with a glass button at the neck and peat-smelling trousers, and the seal-boy with his pelt knotted around his middle now.

There Shelmark told Sigurd the story of Jenny the Witch, which was astonishingly different from the island legend.

17

Shelmark told it so beautifully that when it was over Sigurd clapped his hands and laughed.

'That's only the first cave story,' said Shelmark. 'There's more than a dozen yet to tell. They sound better in the sea, I tell you.'

'I'll swim with you now,' said Sigurd. He dragged his clothes off and ran into the sea. Shelmark the story-teller draped himself in his coat at the sea's edge and leapt through a wave. They swam together into the middle of the Sound. Soon they were joined by the rest of Shelmark's tribe, who swarmed eagerly about their new friend, and touched his cold shoulder with colder snouts. One after the other, in an astonishingly short time, they unfolded to Sigurd in stories the whole history of the cave.

Boys are not at home in the sea like seals. Presently Sigurd's flailing arms grew heavy. 'Shelmark, and you others,' he cried. 'I must go ashore now. I'm very pleased to know you. Thank you for the stories. You must tell me them over and over until I have them by heart.'

On the beach once more, Sigurd had to run about in the sand till sun and wind had dried him enough to let him get his clothes on.

Leaving the shore, he looked seawards. The seal-tribe were clustered about the skerry which was slowly disappearing under the flowing tide. Sigurd waved good-bye to them.

On his way he had to pass the cave. He walked now eagerly into the darkness of it, for Shelmark had touched it with enchantment for him, and he would never be afraid of it again.

'If only we knew the truth about everything that scares us,' thought Sigurd, 'life would be much more bearable.' Even the school, and Mr Prosser and the tawse? Even the Glebe's noisy biting dog? Even the sulphur-and-treacle he had to swallow by the spoonful at the start of each spring to purify his system? Even (thought Sigurd) perhaps them.

He left some whelks he had gathered out of the rockpool at Minnie's door.

When he got home – tired, sun-soaked, smelling of sea – he was in serious trouble.

'Where have you been, my lad?' cried his mother. 'A fine lot of trouble you've created this day! Mr Prosser was here at dinner-time. You never went to the school. Mr Prosser says you're a very difficult boy. What's that on your trousers, seaweed? You never ate your breakfast either. Let me tell you this, I'm having no more trouble from you. To school you'll go tomorrow, if I have to drag you there myself. Is that a *bottle* in your bag?'

His dark strong father sat mildly in the straw-back chair smoking a pipe. He looked grave. He shook his head from time to time. He was a quiet man. He hated any kind of disturbance.

'I'm sorry,' said Sigurd.

'Come and eat your chicken stew,' said his mother. 'You must be starving. Your hair's wet!'

'Yes, mother,' said Sigurd. Some of the sea-magic still clung to him, in spite of the world's disapproval. He went and sat down silently at the table loaded with the goodness of the earth: scones and butter and chicken and potatoes and rhubarb jam.

Jennifer

Jennifer Jane Matilda Stoor was the daughter of the island
minister three hundred years ago. How proud the minister
was of the black-haired beautiful child – what a joy she was
to him in his loneliness (for the mother had died soon after
little Jenny was born).

There was really nothing much for a minister's daughter
to do in the island in those days. The laird and the minister
were the gentry; their children didn't play with the boys and
girls of fishermen and crofters. Stephen Alkirk, the laird's
son, was about the same age as Jenny, but they didn't get on
well together, though Stephen was a pleasant enough lad.

So Jenny grew up a lonely child.

Of course there was no work for her to do in the Manse.

Three servant girls did all that was necessary in the way of cleaning and cooking and lighting the immense fires. They would bow whenever they chanced to pass Miss Jennifer in one of the long corridors. Jenny longed to talk to Bella, Cilla, and Mary (the servant girls) but they knew their place and gave her no encouragement. Often Jenny would hear the three girls laughing and chattering to each other in the kitchen.

Once her father took her on a great adventure, to the General Assembly of the Church in Edinburgh. They stayed with Jenny's aunt, a rather perjink lady called Charlotte. It was, 'Jennifer, your bow is loose!' and 'Jennifer, how often do I have to tell you, you are not to laugh like that in the middle of the High Street!' and 'Sit straight, Jennifer!' from morning to night.

Jenny, now ten, was fascinated by the streets and closes and wynds of the capital, by the gentry with their port-wine faces and the beggars and the swarms of black-coated ministers. She had never seen a carriage before, or a shop. She stood a full five minutes, in utter wonderment, at first sight of the castle on its bold high rock, until Aunt Charlotte said, 'Stop gawking, girl. The people will think you're a simpleton!'

At last, after three weeks, it was over. Jenny and her father took a boat from Leith and sailed home along the east coast of Scotland. They passed fleets of fishing-boats, and off John o' Groats they saw a merchant ship Norway-bound. The sailors waved. Jenny waved back and shouted 'Good luck!' and now there was no Aunt Charlotte to remind her of her dignity. They disembarked at Kirkwall, the Orkney capital.

It was when Jenny saw, from the fishing-boat with the little red sail that was taking them home, the bothies and kirk and scatter of crofts, that she realized how much she loved her island.

She threw her coat over a chair. She burst into the kitchen. 'Bella! Cilla! Mary! I'm home! My dear friends, I'm back again for ever!'

The three scullions, after a few astonished seconds, smiled welcomes to her. Mary went so far as to say, 'We're pleased to see thee, miss.' Then Jenny kissed the rosy country cheeks, all three.

She was out of the big house like a whirlwind. She ran up the hill, and from the summit looked around her. She came dancing down and whirled away towards the shore. It was as if she wanted to embrace the whole island. At the shore there was a seal swimming not far out. She said to the seal, 'I'm home, friend. You can tell the fish and the gulls.'

And the seal replied, 'Welcome home, Jenny. We love you.'

One day two years later the minister said to his daughter, 'Now, Jennifer, my dear, it's time you had some education. This is what I'm planning to do. You remember Edinburgh? You liked that, didn't you? Well, Jennifer, I've enrolled you in a ladies' school in Edinburgh. You're to travel down in a passage-boat immediately after Easter. Charlotte knows – she's making a room all ready for you – the same little room that you slept in before.'

The reverend Mr Stoor – that learned kind man – had never seen such an outburst of temper from his child as erupted then. She would not stay with Aunt Charlotte for a thousand pounds! What did she want with Latin and mathematics and musical scales? She was perfectly happy where she was, in the island. To understand the clouds, and oatfields ripening, and the drift of stars and the drift of seals – that was the wisdom she was interested in. 'I won't – *won't* – WON'T go!' she cried, stamping her foot on the study floor.

The minister was very much perturbed. Most fathers, in those far-off days, would have thrashed their daughters for such rebelliousness; but he put his arm round the sobbing child and comforted her as best he could.

'Oh,' whimpered Jenny, 'if only I had been born in a croft, and knew the right way to milk a cow, and had a herdie-boy for a sweetheart!' . . .

In the end it was decided that Jenny's schooling – for educated she must be, her father was quite determined about that – would be in a room at 'the big house', the Hall of the laird. A tutor, a young divinity student, was brought from Aberdeen. Jenny and Stephen Alkirk shared a desk. Together they learned how to multiply and divide, Latin constructions, some elementary French. As soon as the afternoon's lessons were over, Jenny would rise, curtsy to the tutor, put her books under her arm, and depart.

Stephen Alkirk she never looked at. But Stephen would watch from the school-room window Jenny going home along the road till she was out of sight. If the tutor spoke to him at such a time, he would get only disjointed and way-ward answers.

That summer Jenny was the wildest of all the wild creatures in the island. She flew a kite in the big wind on top of the hill. On warm sunny days she was more often in the sea than on land. Mice ate crumbs and bits of cheese from her hand at the door of the Manse. She shouted from great distances to the shepherd and the crews of fishing boats (and they worked better all that day because of her greeting). 'That girl of mine, Jennifer,' said the minister to the laird one evening over glasses of port, 'she *is* a wild thing! It's as if she gets drunk on wind and sun. Any passing tramp can see her bathing in the rockpools – she doesn't care. I should have

23

insisted on her going to Edinburgh. She would have learned gentility and manners. It's too late now.'

They drank another glass of port, and another, still talking about the problem of Miss Jennifer. The discussion grew deeper and more serious. Finance entered into it. A list of the Orkney gentry was brought out, and discussed, and sifted. It would be possible, thought the laird, to get a ring in Kirkwall; otherwise he would write to a reputable goldsmith in Edinburgh.

When the decanter was empty a winter-time marriage had been arranged between Stephen Alkirk, the laird's son and heir, and Jennifer Jane Matilda Stoor, the minister's only daughter.

Had the good old minister felt a clustering of the shadows about him? It was as if he was anxious, before it was too late, to see his wild daughter made secure and respectable. Perhaps he even hoped to see a little grandson before he closed his eyes for ever . . . The shadows clustered thick and cold about him all that summer. By the time scythes were flashing in the oatfield, the old man lay on the great oak bed of the Manse serene and silent. Jenny folded his hands. A day or two later he was given into the keeping of the earth.

On the road home from the funeral the laird said to Jenny, 'Now, my dear, you realize that there will be another minister appointed to the island at once. That means you must leave the Manse. Well, you are not to worry. We have room and to spare for you at the big house. Your staying with us will in fact be very convenient, in view of the marriage in November.'

There was silence for half-a-mile along the road. Then Jenny said, in the correct style she had learned in the classroom, 'Sir, I have been considering this matter. There will be no marriage, because I do not love your son. I am in love with somebody else. You can inform your son of that.'

The laird stood stock-still on the road. He looked like a man who had been set upon with a club.

'The engagement has been announced,' he breathed. 'The marriage will go on. You are to be the mistress of the Hall.'

'No,' said Jenny, and turned down the little steep shore path that led to the beach. There were other groups of mourners on the road above. Jenny turned from the cliff edge and shouted, 'I won't live in the Manse or the Hall. I have a house of my own. I'm in love with one of God's creatures. The sea will look after me.'

Then a coign of cliff hid her. Her voice was lost in the vast incoming music of the sea.

That was the last that was seen of Jennifer Jane Matilda Stoor in the island. She vanished. She was never seen again.

The island was searched from shore to shore for a full week.

Some people said she had lost her never very robust wits, and drowned herself. But if so, why as the days and weeks passed was no body washed ashore?

Some old superstitious folk began to whisper at the firesides that she was a witch. She had always been a strange creature, hadn't she? Whoever knew of a minister's daughter behaving like her? She spoke to herself on the road – to herself? more likely to her familiar spirit. She seemed to know the languages of gulls and beasts. Fancy any genteel girl encouraging mice with bits of cake at the Manse door! She ate seaweed. She drank salt water. She had vanished (they whispered) and in good time too, before the law had her tried and tortured and burned. Who but a shameless witch would have held up the laird, that great man, to ridicule on the public road, and on such a solemn day as her father's funeral? Some of the wickedest whisperers said she had probably killed the minister with a spell: hadn't the good man wilted like a snowman in April?

The young men of the island, all of whom loved Jenny, wondered that winter in whose lucky arms she was lying. Had a Dutch skipper lifted her from the shore and carried her across the North Sea in his boat? Had she joined the tinker tribe that had been in the island the day she disappeared? If so, she might be anywhere in the straths of Scotland now, or in the bogs of Ireland, lighting ditch fires and selling laces at country doors. The young men couldn't believe such beauty and delight could vanish utterly.

Stephen Alkirk and his tutor (whom the laird had recently appointed to be the new minister) were walking along the cliffs one day the following spring. Below them the sea fell restlessly over rocks and sand. There was a colony of seals on the rock; the mothers were feeding their cubs and the huge bull lay sleepy-eyed in the sun.

The young men discussed predestination and freewill as they strolled along.

Stephen stopped, and pointed. He cried out, 'There she is – Jenny!'

As if in answer to this shout the seal tribe rolled and trundled from the skerry. The Sound was full of little splashes. They drifted out to sea.

One seal-face turned and looked back at the island of wicked old witch whispers and young broken hearts.

If you're not scared to go into the cave, you can see (once your eyes grow accustomed to the gloom) the chamber where Jenny lived in the six days before her sea bridal. There's the ledge where she sat, and the little pool where she washed her face, and afterwards (when it grew still and lucent again) combed out her long black hair. She went to sleep night after night with the music of the sea all around. And there, on the day appointed, her lover came with the sealskin to claim a bride.

The seals of this island are all Jenny's children.

Stone people

The history of the cave is much older than Jennifer Jane Matilda Stoor.

Think of a little pastoral village on the west side of the island – a cluster of stone houses linked by narrow stone wynds. Everything was made of stone, the beds and the cupboards and the doors. There were no trees on the island then; there had been forests once, but in this cold time those branches and roots had long melted into the peat-mosses. The villagers had never heard of iron and bronze. They used the only material that lay plentifully everywhere about them: stone.

Very skilful were the quarriers, the masons, the stone 'carpenters'. Like enough every boy in the village learned to be a stone worker, as well as a shepherd and hunter and fisherman. The village was too small for separate trades, and the population had too precarious a foothold in time. An epidemic, or a raid, could conceivably wipe out the community. So each man knew all the skills of the village; in case of disaster, a single survivor and his mate could ensure a continuance of some kind.

What did the women do? What women have always done: borne children, and comforted the sick, and shrouded the dead. They lit fires and fetched water. They knew what herbs, in what proportion, were good against this sickness and that. Old, they muttered half-forgotten wisdom in the smoke of winter fires. Young, they delighted in shells and rockpools, and made combs out of sheep bone.

The villagers knew nothing about ploughs and corn. They never ventured far out in their frail skin-covered boats. They would say to the seals, 'Don't eat too many fish. Leave some of them for us.' They would say to the sheep, 'Are you not weary of life? You must be tired of munching that thin grass. Listen, sheep. We are cold and we are hungry. Help us. Forgive us.' Then they would kill a sheep with their stone knives. They would say to the fish, 'Now, then, you are going a journey with us. We are taking you home to our village. We will make you very welcome, haddocks. The women will honour you. They'll make a brightness out of your liver, oil for lamps. They'll make a sharpness out of your bones, needles for our skin coats. They make fish very sweet in the nostrils and in the mouth, our women.'

The children would sing to the seals all summer long.

Once a young man, gathering shore stones, saw a ship on the horizon. He ran home and panted out the news. The villagers gathered everything of value – sheep, tools, skins, oars – and went silently inland like clouds. One old man was too feeble to go. 'Leave me,' he said. 'I still know how to say black words. Perhaps the strangers will turn away from the curse I lay on them. The curse has great power. More likely they will kill me and kick me out of the way and then search for our precious things. Leave me. There are only a few more months left to me in any case.'

The strange sail fluttered on the horizon, the bow probed in towards the bay and the deserted village. No doubt the sailors could see that the coast was inhabited. Nearer the boat drifted. Dark frightened eyes watched from the hills. But then suddenly, towards noon, the sail fluttered again, and the boat turned north. The villagers could see the red and black beards of the sailors, and the gleam from the arm of him who sat in the prow, a shining circle brighter than the sun. Once the boat was behind the cliff the people rose from their hiding-places and shouted with relief and joy. They ran and danced all the way back to the village. A whole morning had been wasted, but there might still be time to catch a few fish before sunset. The old man was squatting where they had left him in the village square. He thought the approaching feet were the strangers' feet. He thought their laughter was the strangers' laughter. He said: 'The curse fall on your hands and on your hair. May the curse cripple you. May the curse sink you. Barrenness be in the curse, and death, and the death of the imagination that looks beyond death.' ... 'Grand-dad,' said a boy, 'it's us, your friends. The strangers have sailed on northwards. Now bless us.'

It was too late. The curse had been put irremovably upon the village and its people. They could see no way of avoiding it.

The old man cried out in chagrin and fear. That same night he died.

The curse remained with the villagers. How would the end

come? Very likely that ship was but the first of many, a spy ship sent on before to seek out suitable islands for settling in. A dozen ships would follow in the next moon. The sailors would smoke out every village along the coast. Then, once the islands were theirs, they would take out their crooked wood and wound the earth. That had happened in other places in the knowledge of the present generation of villagers: fleets of dark men from the south, burning, stealing, destroying, wounding the earth in that mysterious way.

Or perhaps the curse would work this way: the men from another more populous village would come one day and stand on the beach. They would say, 'Too many of our women have died this spring. Give us, friends, a dozen of your best and most fruitful women.' The villagers would say nothing. Then the petitioners would advance up the beach. They would seize this woman or that, and drag her down by the hair. Then the villagers, with cries of pity, would run to plead for the home-biding safety of their girls. The despoilers would turn on them and kill them all, even the boys and the old toothless men, and the raging women would be thrown into the boats.

The villagers had known such a thing to happen in other places.

Or perhaps, to fulfil the curse, the seals would say, 'The voice of your children enchant us. We will take them to sing to us at the bottom of the sea.' So, without a posterity, the ageing village would perish at last.

Or perhaps the fish would say, 'You villagers have gulled us too long. Gather us home, would you? Make lamp-oil out of us, and needles, and a sweetness in the nostrils and the mouth? It was all lies, deception, death.' And the fish would call upon the element they lived in, the sea, to rise about the doors of the village, and higher still, even up to the lintel – so that those lying villagers would know the kind of living streams a fish breathes and flourishes in. The end might come in that way. The villagers had heard of floods in former times.

In fact the end came the following winter, and after quite another fashion.

Winter fell black and stormy over the islands. But the villagers were well prepared for that. They had their lamps and their peatfires, and enough dried fish and mutton to see them through to the spring. In winter the old ones came into their own, those too feeble to fish and herd. Their mouths brimmed all night with the stories of the tribe, and very ancient songs. A few old men and women were the custodians of the tribe's wisdom; after the laughter and the music and the dancing, phrases from the sacred lore, uttered by withered voices, held the villagers in wonderment.

On this last night they could hear the wind prowling about the streets of the village, and the whisper of blown sand on the turf roofs. But their ears were intent on a more entrancing thing, old Bonda telling a story about their gods. All the villagers were in the chief's house, except a young man called Iffling who said he was going out to see that the boats were all right in the rising wind.

'The god of the earth has a stone face. He is not to be moved. The god of the earth has many lovers who seek him out to be loved by them. The sea loves the earth god. "Look," she cried once, "I am washing your feet, I am kissing your hands. I am stronger than you, in the end I will break down your cliffs. Then we will be lovers." '

The young man Iffling entered from outside and said that the wind was rising still from the north-west. He had stowed the boats in a sheltered place. It was a terrible night. He could not see the far side of the bay for blown sand.

Affronted faces looked round at Iffling. How dared he

disturb the beautiful story? Rebuked, Iffling returned into the loud black night.

'The god of the earth has a stone face and is not to be moved. The god has many lovers but he has no love for any of them. Fire loves the earth god. "I will make you beautiful coats of red. I will sew yellow coats for you." The earth god is angry with fire. Fire burns him with red pain, whenever the mood of loving is on her. 'Keep to the houses of my children called men,' the earth god says to fire. "Be their slaves and servants. That's what I think of you." '

Iffling entered again; his eyes were hidden with hair and spume and sand. 'The beach is moving!' he cried. 'The beach is trampling on us!'

This time they *had* to pay attention to him. Iffling was a brave practical young fellow. They had not seen him like this before, on the edge of hysteria. A few men followed Iffling out into the street with covered heads. The street was a long curving howl. There was a sinister noise outside that the villagers had never heard before – a rasping and whooping in the air. More folk stooped out through the low door. They gathered their children. If there was to be danger, they would face it in their own houses.

Iffling's voice, resolute now, came wind-broken from the bank above the village. 'There's no time to save anything. The village is choking to death. Every man and woman and child must make his own way to the great cave. That's the only sheltered place on a night like this. Hurry!'

Bonda sat alone in the sand-blanketed village.

'The stone face of the earth god seeks no kisses. Sky loves the earth god. "See," she cries, "I shower you with gifts. There's no end to the love I have for you. Here is light, take that. Here is a golden cup, I call it the sun, take that. Here is a lamp, I call it the moon, its wick goes up and down, that lamp, earth god. Here are my million pearls of dew, take them also for a present. What, you are dirty from the hunt! Wash in my sweet rain, you dear one. You are tired, you are weary with growing grass and plants all summer for your beasts to feed on, you want to sleep. For your sleeping time I have made a roof of darkness and I have woven for your winter bed a white coverlet of snow. And still, cruel one, you will not let me lie beside you." '

Bonda told the story to the end, though there was no one to hear her. The domestic fire raged like a beast on its imprisoning stone. Outside the wind was a mad gravedigger hastening to bury the village in a grave of sand. The stonework groaned. Old Bonda sat quiet, having told her story, and folded her hands.

Many of the villagers never reached the cave. Some were blown by the storm over the cliffs. Some of the old ones lay down and died on the moss. The survivors could do nothing about that. Heads into wind, the strongest ones stumbled on, carrying children and an occasional sheep in their arms.

At last, singly or in groups, they came to the sheltered side of the hill. There was a pathway down the crag. In the darkness they felt their way down. There was a huge black mouth in the cliff: the cave. They entered it, cold and accursed.

More villagers were dead of exposure before a grey dawn broke. Hardly any children survived that terrible night. And still the storm howled over the island.

The next day, the men managed to gather enough kindling to make a fire. They killed one of the sheep and roasted it. Iffling's mother died among the smoke. The storm went on for three days. Another child died; the little body, blue with cold, was wrapped in the scarlet of fire.

'Let us go back to the village,' said a man. 'The wind has shifted a little.'

Iffling disappeared that morning. The people were

terrified that he, their best young man, had been taken by the huge seas. But Iffling came back, before dark. 'I went to the village,' he said. 'It is not there. There is nothing but humps of sand.'

They were accustomed to stone, the villagers, but friendly stone, stone into which their imaginations had entered (the fire-stone, the food-stone, the sleeping-stone), not to this cold jagged hostile orifice in the cliff. The cave had not received them like a mother.

One morning the seven survivors woke in the cave to a tranced silence. The long storm was over. The air was blue and lucent, but the sea remembered the tempest and still sent its waves crashing down on the stones and sand outside. The cave-dwellers smiled to each other; now they could see to the making of a new village. The tribe would not die after all.

Later that morning they saw against the horizon half-a-dozen ships sailing north. What they had suspected was true – the first ship had been only a forerunner, a seeker-out of fertile places. Now strangers were coming in strength to occupy the islands. Would the strangers suffer the gentle stone-people to carry on with their fishing and shepherding on the coast? The stone-people had heard about the cruelty of those adventurers. They would laugh at the stone clubs and flint arrowheads. The ship-men were clever and ruthless; they had learned how to burrow into the mountains for ore – their axes glittered and clanged, and made terrible wounds.

In the afternoon twelve more ships sailed north in a cluster. 'It is a great migration,' said Iffling. 'They will break open all the stone villages of Orkney. Our day is done.'

That night in the cave they ate the last of the mutton. Over the fire they told each other as many of the stories and bits of wisdom as they could remember, and they laughed to each other across the fire.

In the first light of morning three more ships sailed black along the horizon. Their wings fluttered. They stood in to shore.

'Now,' said Iffling, 'we could fish on such a fine morning, but we have no boats. I am tired of eating seaweed. Shall we die of cold and starvation in this cave? That is a poor end to our people. Answer me.'

The young men and women had nothing to say.

Iffling said, 'Those three ships will make landfall on the bay where we used to live. What will we do – return to our shore, take them by the beards, drown them in the breakers? We will not. We are a mild people. They are stronger than us.'

The six were silent still.

'We will go to the sailors,' said Iffling, 'and stretch our hands to them. We will welcome them to our island. There are secrets in our sky and sea that we can show them. We will tell them some of the old stories. Perhaps they will be glad of our friendship.'

They shook their heads.

'At any rate,' said Iffling, 'I am curious about their pieces of curved wood that they wound the earth with. I have heard that out of the wounds, at the end of summer, comes a sweeter pleasanter surer food than the flesh of sheep or fish. We will lie among the grass and watch the strangers dragging their boats up the sand. We will look at the bright rings on their arms. We will hear a strange honeyed language. Then, when they come up against some difficulty – such as the finding of the water springs, which only we can tell them – we will rise up from the long grass, and call, and hold out our hands to them.'

The six followed Iffling out of the cave, slowly. They trudged up to the headland.

They could see the red and black beards on the homing ships, and the bright circle on the arm of the tall man in the prow of the leading ship.

The ship of death

The great one of the island was dead. He lay in the long hall, hushed and cold. Down at the beach they began to make preparations for his funeral, for his last voyage. The people came from all over the island with bits of driftwood (the Orkneys are treeless) and basketfuls of peat. The poorest brought bundles of dry heather to make torches.

There were two men – father and son – who had skill in building with stone. They were sent for. They set to work down at the Bay of Seals. They began to gather stones into the cave. It was too cold and stormy to work on the open beach.

When a great king or Viking chief died in the north his body was laid in the well of a funeral ship. Perhaps in the earliest days this ship with its body and all its accoutrements of war and rank was actually launched into the tidestreams. Then from the small boats the torches were thrown in. The flaming ship of death drifted westwards. All that could be seen at last was the red glare on the horizon; then darkness and silence. The great one was making his last voyage.

Then after many generations 'the last voyage' became less realistic. A symbolical ship was built on the shore. The dead chief was laid in it with his sword and axe and the silver he had robbed from Irish churches. Then the torches were thrown in, amid cries of farewell and fragments of heroic poetry and dancing among the flames. Through a great wave of fire the hero was cast on Valhalla.

But this little island was too poor for such ceremony. Wood was scarce and dear; it had to be brought from Norway and Scotland for their houses and fishing boats. Besides, their chief did not count among the great councillors. Sometimes the Earl of Orkney did not even bother to send for him when he summoned an all-island assembly at his great hall in Birsay. He ate the same food as his people and often in spring he was as hungry as them, and was glad of a few shellfish on his table. He certainly could not afford to sail a ship among the Viking fleet that set out each spring, after the ploughing and seed-time, to harry the coasts of Scotland, England, and France.

Now he was dead, an old quiet farmer, the father of the island. His son was there to succeed him, a dark grasping man. The islanders did not look forward to the levying of the next year's rents.

Nobody wept for a death. A life-time is something endured and achieved. There ought to be rejoicing when the work is finished. They believed that the best way for a man to die was in a battle or a siege or a shipwreck. Then he passed on at once to 'the hall of the immortal heroes'. But if he had the misfortune to be unblessed by storm or axe, and withered into old age, and died by reason of wheeziness or a blood-flux, even so the last act of all should have a heroic seal put on it.

In the cave the masons set stone upon stone in the form of a ship. When you stood close to this stone ship it was a rather crude piece of workmanship. The workers had had great difficulty, for example, in reproducing in stone the proud swell of a hull. But viewed from the lowest reach of the ebb and in the cave-gloom, it looked well enough. Of course the builders had not even attempted to rear a mast.

When the two men finally stood back from their stone ship and dusted their hands, the islanders put their fuel on board – driftwood and peat. They arranged the kindling with great care.

The wind had begun to blow cold again from the north.

Then from the long hall the body was brought down. He had been a quiet farmer all his days, but now on this last day of all he was a hero. The chief was dressed in his best coat and shoes and hat. They laid him on top of the pyre. There was a good deal of laughter and joking. 'You crafty old one, slipping away from us as suddenly as that.' ... 'You'll be drunk tonight in the hall of Valhalla.' ... 'What lies are you going to tell the heroes and the kings, Thord?'

Then by his side they set the axe and the sword that were red with rust because the old chief had never had occasion to redden them with more heroic stuff.

On his breast they spread the only bit of treasure in the hall – a small tapestry of a hawk on a tower that the earl had given him once on one of his rare visits to the island.

They saw that the dead chief was smiling, as if he approved of what was being done, as if he relished the great voyage before him – the only voyage, in fact, that he had ever made.

As if to emphasize the heroic element of this funeral, the worst gale of the winter began to howl over the island. The islanders could hardly hear each other speaking. The birds flew between sea and cloud in wild torn circles. When the new chief tried to light the first torch of heather on the beach the flame would not take.

Finally they had to go into the shelter of the cave to light the dozen torches. The sun went down in the west in a red-and-black smoulder. That was the time – nightfall – for a hero to set out on his last voyage.

The wind threw the flames about – in one or two cases extinguished them. Then the torches were thrust into the kindling. The flames congregated in the pyre, whispered and crepitated, then broke out, raged and sang and leaped in the wind, and climbed, until it seemed that a silken sail of yellow and scarlet was shaking out. The dead man lay glorified in the flames for a second or two.

The beautiful ceremony was soon over. The sail of fire dwindled. The burning body collapsed through the charred pyre. It seethed among the coals and embers.

'Farewell!' shouted the islanders outside the cave. 'Well done, old one!' . . . 'A good voyage, hero.' . . .

The children danced and laughed about the last of the fire, and the blackened ship, and the simmering bones.

The islanders would have stayed there till morning, in honour of their dead chief. It was when they heard the surly voice of the new chief that they knew there were harder times before them. 'I suppose you'll all be wanting drink now. There's always ale at a funeral. Well, the women have brewed a pot or two. Don't imagine you can make a night of it up at the Hall. One drink and home you go. I'm a poor man. My father was too lax altogether. This island will have to work a lot harder from now on.'

Spider's kingdom

A man stood alone on the north shore of Strathnaver. This was almost the world's end, but not quite. To the north-east two blue hills reared out of the sea – the island of Hoy in Orkney. Further north, well under the horizon, were the Shetland Islands. 'And all these lands,' said the man, 'belong rightly to the kingdom of Scotland.'

He heard hooves in the strath behind him. He listened; after a while the echoes died away. It was possible that those horsemen were his enemies, and were looking for him. He went quickly down to the shore where a few fishermen were getting their boats ready.

The man said to the most reliable-looking of the fishermen, an elderly man with gentle eyes and a dark grey-flecked beard, 'Is it the lobsters you're after today?'

The fisherman nodded.

The others stopped their work to listen. They looked at the stranger with curiosity and some hostility. These were dangerous times in Scotland; the countryside had its quota of spies. To say a wrong word could cost a man his life.

'I have business in the Orkneys,' said the man. 'You would do me a great favour to sail me there in your boat.'

The fisherman said that a very dangerous stretch of water, the Pentland Firth, lay between Scotland and Orkney. He doubted if his boat could endure those torn and whirling waters. Besides, he had six children at home, and a wife, and he must see to their hungers.

The stranger took a coin out of his purse and held it up. The sun flashed from it. It was a gold coin, the first that the fisherman had ever seen.

'Here is the fare,' said the stranger. 'It is yours as soon as you set me down on an Orkney shore.'

The fisherman said, 'Sit quietly in the stern all the way. Don't move or you'll upset the boat. Don't speak even – I'll be wanting all my concentration to navigate.'

The stranger helped the fisherman to push the boat down into the sea.

They were just clearing the headland when a woman appeared on the shore and shouted to them. She had a fierce shrill voice. 'What's this I hear?' she yelled. 'Taking a passenger to Orkney, are you? Come back here, man, or I'll warm your lugs with my fists. A widow and six orphans – that's what we'll be if you go among those waters! Turn the boat round.'

'That's my wife,' said the fisherman, and he kept the bow pointed north. 'She has opinions of her own.'

'I would be frightened,' said the stranger, 'if I was tied to a formidable woman like her.'

'I *am* frightened,' said the fisherman. 'I'm as frightened of her as I am of the Pentland Firth. But I'm hoping that when she sees that golden mark her anger will turn to kisses.'

It turned out that the stranger's estimate of the fisherman was correct – he was a careful reliable boatman. Once out at sea he hoisted a sail and held west.

'I am not wanting to go to Atlantis,' said the stranger.

'Be quiet,' said the fisherman. 'I told you not to speak.'

Soon they were in the grip of the eastering tide-race. The boat rocked to a new dangerous rhythm. The sea was whorled and dimpled like the bottoms of immense bottles. The fisherman sat in the stern, his strong fist on the tiller. The bow reared north, then north-east, with great plungings and showers of spindrift. It ettled, and steadied, and held that course. 'I am keeping to the edge of the tide,' said the fisherman. 'The tide is our friend now – it is carrying us fast to Orkney.'

The stranger said nothing. He gazed, with sorrow and pride, at the receding coast of Scotland.

Soon they were in calmer water, and the face of the fisherman relaxed. He looked with open curiosity at his passenger. What was the man wanting in these distant parts? He was too well-dressed to be a wandering holy man. He was too honest-looking to be a merchant. It was – the fisherman could see – a face that had suffered; but the fires it had been in had only served to harden an innate authority and resolution.

The red western cliff-lines of Orkney came nearer and nearer. 'What island would you be wanting to go to?' said the fisherman.

The man continued to gaze back at the faint bluish coast of Scotland, and the diminishing mountains. 'When I come back to you, dear land,' he said, 'there will be a different story to tell.'

The fisherman, now that the danger was finally past, tried by subtle questionings to find out who the stranger was, and what his business was in these Norwegian-governed islands. Had he friends there? Would he be staying there for the rest of the summer? His wife, now, she would be missing him, in their house in Stirling, or Perth, or Edinburgh. (And he hoped she had a sweeter tongue than his own bread-baker.) Ah, business led a man into many a remote place. All the same, he did not think his passenger could be a merchant – he would guess, if he was asked, that he must be a scrivener, he had the kind of hands on him that turned pages and wielded quill pens. One thing was certain – hands like those had never gripped the stilts of a plough or sunk creels in the cold ocean. But on the whole, said the fisherman, as the bird-circling cliffs of the island loomed above them, he thought the stranger must be a skilled craftsman – a tapestry-maker perhaps or a master mason – who had been summoned north to do some specialized task for the Earl of Orkney.

The man said nothing.

The keel grated on the stones of the island shore. The stranger opened his purse again and gave the gold coin to his ferryman, and thanked him. Then he put his hand on the bow and vaulted lightly ashore.

Once on the sand he turned again and said to the fisherman, 'I think you were making inquiries much of the time, in a discreet but devious way, as to my occupation. Fisherman, I am your king.'

The man who claimed to be the king of Scotland walked slowly through the island. He met no one, but he was aware of eyes watching him from corners and croft doors. There was one large house in the centre of the island among a scattering of poor houses (in which the same roofs sheltered people and animals). The hay harvest was in full swing in the field next the big house. Every man in the island had been summoned to labour with hayfork and ox, and the overseer kept them hard at work. He was a broad-shoul-dered swarthy man, forever shouting and running hither and thither, and occasionally boxing a harvester on the ear. The haystack grew, shaggy and shaking in the wind.

The stranger crossed the field and said to the overseer, 'Man, I would be glad if you would tell your master I want a few words with him.'

The overseer shook his head – it was obvious he did not understand – the Scots tongue was foreign to him. The har-vesters stopped working and looked long and wonderingly at the stranger.

The overseer noticed that his labourers were letting their sweat dry on them. He turned. 'What in hell's wrong with you!' he shouted in the Norn tongue. 'Get on with your work. Haven't you seen a vagrant before? The haystack must be built and secured before the sun goes down.'

The stranger did not understand this northern language; but there was little need for that; the violent mime of the overseer, his assault and battery on the three harvesters in his immediate vicinity, illustrated his meaning only too viv-idly. The men covered their heads with their arms. The over-seer ran at a fourth one and kicked him on the behind.

The door of the big house opened and a well-dressed man came out, no doubt drawn by the uproar.

'That's enough, Nord,' he said sternly. 'You won't get much work out of cripples. That's what you'll make them all, man, if you carry on like that.'

Then the speaker, who was obviously the chief man in the island, noticed the stranger. He said ungraciously in Scots (as if the stranger had a southern look about him), 'Who are you? What do you want?'

The stranger said, 'I have had to leave my home and my people for a while. I have been driven out of Scotland by my enemies. I will go back again, and secure my inheritance. But just now it is not safe. The English are everywhere in Scotland. Here I can be safe for a month or two, or maybe longer. I need peace and leisure to make my plans. That's impossible while I'm being hunted here and there, and informed on by traitors. If you would give me shelter and lodging in your house, sir, in the end it would be a matter of great fame and honour to you.'

'Fame and honour!' cried the chief. 'Fame and honour for sheltering a man I've never cast eyes on before, a fugitive. What man of majesty and might has deigned to visit my island? I would advise you to be out of this island before dark. We don't like vagabonds here.'

The overseer, now that the haystack was busy as a beehive again, added his black scowl to the discourtesy of his lord.

'I might let you sleep in the byre till tomorrow,' said the farmer after a while. 'Among the beasts. How will you pay? Can you sing? Can you work in the hayfield? For I'm sure you have no money.'

'I gave my last gold coin to the boatman who sailed me here from Scotland. You will be well paid when I come into my inheritance. It happens that I am the king of Scotland.'

Thereupon the farmer, after a first gape of astonishment, abandoned himself to mirth. He bent double with laughter. He straightened himself and clasped his side with both hands. He became red in the face and tears flowed from the slits of his eyes. His great thunders of mirth caused another interruption in the work of the harvesters. Several of them began to laugh too (though they couldn't tell why); one was so convulsed he fell off the stack. The only islander uninfected by the general merriment was the morose overseer.

The stranger stood gravely in the middle of this gale of mockery.

At last the farmer's spasms ended in a wheeze, and watery eyes, and a shaking forefinger.

'The king of Scotland!' he said weakly. 'O Lord, I thought I had heard everything – the last ebb of delusion – when that old mad tramp came here last Yule. He said he was the Earl of Thule, come to pay me a friendly visit over the twelve days of the feast. I soon sent *him* packing!'

'We put the dogs on him,' said the overseer darkly.

'You've gone one better,' said the chief to the stranger. 'The king of Scotland indeed! Next it'll be the Pope of Rome himself seeking my hospitality.'

'I am the king of Scotland,' said the man.

'Listen, friend,' said the chief. 'You will be out of this island by sunset. I do not entertain liars or madmen. See to it.'

He turned and stumped back slowly into his house.

'Go back the way you came,' said the overseer in his incomprehensible tongue, but the stranger could read the vindictiveness in his face and bearing.

He turned back towards the shore.

The man who claimed to be king of Scotland said to the seals clustering about the skerry, 'This is a great wonder to me, that beasts can be milder and more welcoming than men.'

He went into the cave. 'I've been in many a hovel in the last ten years and more,' he said, 'but this is the coldest and roughest shelter of all. A hard couch. A bare cupboard.'

It was still only late afternoon, hardly the time to stretch out on his stony bed. Besides, he would have to be vigilant.

He wouldn't put it past that island chief to have him followed, and, if found, beaten or even murdered.

'This is the lowest point in my fortunes,' said the stranger to seals and seabirds. 'I have fallen so low that I may never be able to get out of this pit. Six times I've tried to assert my right to my kingdom – six times the crown has turned to ashes in my hands. Six times is enough, I think. There comes an end to a man's striving and ingenuity. As for my luck, the last of that seems to have run out. It may be that I will never leave this cave. Who would sail me to Shetland from this island? They will find next winter a long skeleton among the stones. They will wonder at the royal ring on its finger.'

All the while he was speaking the stranger saw, in a niche of a cave, a spinning spider. The insect was having poor luck with its web. For one thing, draughty rock is not the best foundation for a structure so delicate. A stray gust blew the web down when it was almost finished. Another time a dollop of water was shaken from the roof of the cave and made a rupture. Once indeed the stranger himself, in a quirk of absent-mindedness, poked a stick into the web and ruined it. Another time a freighted bee blundered into it and left a shambles. Whatever evil end its labours had, the spider refused to be beaten. There was endless patience and determination in that tiny architect. Out it swung on its trapeze, once more the first bit of silver scaffolding was fixed to the inhospitable cave niche, and the intricate frail construction got under way again. Six times the airy house collapsed, for one reason or another, just when it seemed that the work had been finally accomplished. The sun was down, the light was fading. Soon the spider, like the stranger, would be benighted and destitute. It swung and clambered and fell and climbed and crossed, all the time spinning the stuff of life out of itself; and, when the only light in the cave was the sky-gleam reflected from a rockpool, the spider's house was finished. The man looked, and saw that it was good. 'Well done, fellow-mortal,' he said, and clapped his hands.

He took a dagger from his belt and laid it beside his stone pillow. Then he stretched himself out to sleep.

In the morning the stranger was up and stirring early. He must try to be away from this dangerous island soon, though how he could not guess.

Perhaps, if he walked round to the west, he might attract some fishing-boat or cargo-boat Scotland-bound. On a promontory he came suddenly on a small monastery.

'Well,' he said, 'to think that I spent a whole night in a cave, when I could have had sanctuary with the brothers!'

He clambered up the sea-bank towards the monastery. He did not want to meet any of the hostile islanders. But this morning they were sleeping long after their labours in the hayfield.

He knocked on the monastery door. The doorkeeper opened. 'Welcome, stranger,' he said. 'You look tired and hungry. We're just going to eat, between Matins and Lauds. Come inside.'

The stranger entered the refectory. Twelve bald heads bowed to him, twenty-four hands were folded dove-like. A place was made for him next to the abbot. A hidden voice sang the thanks of the community for the bread and fish and milk on the table.

'Now, my son,' said the abbot. 'Eat in peace. Speak if you want to speak. We don't get many visitors in this lonely place, and so we don't know what's happening in the big busy world outside. We don't greatly care either. So, friend, if you want to tell us who you are, and what you're doing here, and what adventures you've had and what people you've met, we will listen with interest. But if not, bless your silence.'

The stranger thanked them for a kindly welcome. Then he said that he was the king of Scotland.

Heads bent over their meagre plates, they showed no astonishment. They nodded, smiling.

He told them that, a dozen years previously, the king of England had asserted his domination over Scotland. At last the people had rebelled, led by a brave knight, Sir William Wallace. This patriot had been taken by treachery, and barbarously done to death by the hangman in London. Then it seemed that King Edward of England had Scotland at his feet; the speaker himself, though a Scot, was at that time one of King Edward's men. But the woe and degradation heaped on his people, year by year, turned him into a patriot at last. The Scottish magnates – or some of them – flocked about him. In Scone he had been crowned king by the archbishop. But that, alas, was not the happy end of the story by any means. Enmity, envy, malice – from his own countrymen more than from the Saxon castle-keepers – thwarted him at every turn. Finally, after six vain efforts to assert his kingship, he had left Scotland in utter discouragement; not to her fate, but to contemplate at a safe remove either the blossoming of the thistle or its withering. (Often, at the centre of affairs, there is too much melling, sweat, confusion.)

'You understand,' said the abbot, 'we don't ask here whether a man is a king or a beggar. It's sufficient that he is an immortal soul. The Kingdom of Heaven is of more concern to us than Scotland or England or Norway. This much I grant – a man can work and pray better if he is a free man in a free country.'

A monk sang Latin out of a book on the lectern. The brothers broke the bread in front of them. The abbot listened to his guest, his head tilted, smiling.

'At yesterday's sunset,' said the stranger, 'I was beaten. I

51

acknowledged it. I could do no more. I was the broken king of a broken country.'

'You can stay here,' said the abbot, 'until you decide what is best for you to do. You can stay here for a year. You can stay for ever. Of course you would have to fish from the rock, and learn to plough. Every man must labour to the glory of God.'

'I will accept your hospitality for one night only,' said the stranger. 'I intend to go back to Scotland. Last night the wisdom of the spider entered into me.'

The brothers nodded and smiled all about him.

'Indeed,' said the abbot, 'the creatures have a great deal to teach us. We have a book in our library here full of animal legends – a bestiary – it has the most exquisite drawings in it. It was illuminated in Ireland four hundred years ago. There is no spider-legend in it, though.'

'I will tell you one now,' said the stranger. 'Do you have a good scribe in your monastery? Perhaps, if there's a blank page in your bestiary, some day when he has an hour to spare, he will write it down.' Then he told the abbot about the cave and that invincible spider.

The brothers ate in silence except for the mild chant of the lector reading a fragment from the life of a saint.

'Now,' said the abbot, dipping his fingers in a bowl of water and wiping them, 'I do not know the rights and wrongs of the political situation in that huge island to the south where two nations are housed in enmity, Scotland and England. Whether it's best that the island remain divided, or that it be welded together in one nation – I have no opinion in the matter. But it's certain – you know this better than us, with our psalters and our candles – that either the cleaving or the joining together (whichever is more just in the eye of heaven) will be accomplished only with blood and fire and much suffering. And will you go back into that smithy of war for the seventh time?'

'I will,' said the stranger. 'Tomorrow.'

'Brother Anselm will sail you across in our fishing boat,' said the abbot. 'In the morning, after Matins. Go in peace into your sevenfold war. Anselm is the best boatman in Orkney.'

Before he sailed back to Scotland, the abbot gave King Robert Bruce a box with a relic of the Orkney martyr, Saint Magnus, in it.

That relic was carried by the Scottish army into the last battle of the war, fought under Stirling Castle, in midsummer 1314. The famous English archers were cut down early by the Scottish horsemen; the finest chivalry of England wallowed in the pits that had been dug for them on prepared ground. The cavalry of King Edward the Second broke on the hedgehog-shaped 'schildrons' of the Scottish infantry. The remnants of the huge invading army fled from the Scottish camp-followers that came swarming down the hill towards sunset, to discover what loot there might be.

At the end of that famous day King Robert finished the web-spinning, and his kingdom was established.

The man from the Armada

For three days and nights a great gale from the west blew over the islands. The fishing boats lay furled and fastened on the beach. If a crofter ventured out to see to his thatch or his haystack, the wind would lead him a fine dance before he managed to stagger back to his own threshold again. The grass was salted. The air was flecked with drifting spume. The whole island trembled to the terrible music of the sea against the high western cliffs of the island.

'Anna,' said the old man in the wooden shut-bed, 'is everything all right about the place?'

'Yes, Father,' said Anna, 'I took in enough peats to last for a week. There's a bucket of water left. The beasts are contented among the straw. Only the horse gets a bit nervous sometimes when there's a howl in the wind that only he can hear.'

'I'm tired of life,' said the old man. 'I pray to be dead.'

That was the way all conversations between father and daughter had ended for the past six months – a self-pitying prayer for oblivion. He had been a cheerful active man all his days. Then one day in March he had fallen among the furrows and broken a leg. That had been the end of him. Three crofters had carried him up to his wooden bed, and there he had lain ever since, sighing and complaining and begging for the end.

Anna did what she could for him. It was a hard life for her – working the croft, cooking and spinning, attending to a helpless invalid. But she was a cheerful girl (if rather plain-featured). She was happy enough so long as she could get outside in the wind and sun, away from the constant hopeless complainings from the box-bed.

'The wind,' thought Anna as she swept a scatter of ashes on the hearth, 'is not so loud now on the gable-end as it was an hour ago.'

'Anna,' said the old man.

'I'm listening, Daddo,' she answered.

'I ask God,' said the old man, 'why did he give me a plain-looking lass and not a son who would work this croft after I'm gone, which won't be long now, thank goodness.'

'I don't know,' said the girl.

'Your looks won't get you a husband,' said the old man. 'Mary and Jemima and Armingert from this same hillside are all married and they're younger than you. Are you listening?'

'Yes, Daddo,' said Anna.

The old man pointed to the opposite stone wall. 'Do you see a stone there with no cement round it?' he said. 'A hand's-breadth from the water-niche.'

'I think so, said Anna.

'Well,' said the crofter, 'nobody knows about it but myself. That stone comes out. Inside you'll find a piece of sacking. Undo the knot, and you'll find three silver crowns.'

'I won't touch it while you're alive,' said Anna.

'You'll do what I say,' said her father. 'This very evening you'll take that money in your hand and you'll go to the croft of Smelt where Thord lives. Wash your face first. Put on your best shawl and a decent pair of shoes. When Thord comes to the door, you're to say nothing to him at all. Most women put their foot in it as soon as they speak. You will bow your head. You will open your fist. In your palm the three crowns will be lying. Thord is a greedy man. He'll understand that language well enough.'

The girl said nothing.

'Thord's no fool,' said the old man. 'He knows you're a hard-working good-natured lass. Beauty means nothing to Thord. He knows that this croft will soon have no tenant. For me, that time can't come soon enough.'

Anna said she thought the storm was blowing itself out at last.

'Well,' said her father, 'what are you waiting for? Take the stone out of the wall. Aren't you anxious to see your dowry-money?'

'I'm going to bake some scones now,' said Anna. 'Then I'll go next door and milk the cow. Scones-and-honey with milk – you'll like that, Daddo.'

'You're a wicked girl!' cried the old man. 'If I haven't enough to suffer, without this hard-heartedness! Can't I be allowed to die in peace, at least? You are to marry Thord Sinclair of Smelt. Bring the money here to me.'

Anna had great affection for her father, and great pity for him also since his fall among the furrows. She hated to hurt him with disobedience and flat denial. (One thing she was determined about, she would never become the wife of Thord Sinclair, a coarse brutal man who – it was said – had driven his poor drudge to an early grave.)

The crisis in the little hillside croft was mercifully interrupted by a loud knocking at the door and a lifting of the latch. A well-known face appeared, old Katrin who carried news from one end of the island to the other, and specialized in scandal and everything outrageous.

'Come in, Katrin!' cried Anna in a more welcoming voice than she usually accorded the tale-bearer.

The old man groaned and mumbled in his bed.

The gossip-monger, storm-buffeted, leaned against the door-post. 'O Lord,' she wheezed, 'wait till I get my breath.'

This was the first face that Anna had seen since the great storm began. It was a sign indeed that the winds were wilting. Through the door that Katrin had left half open Anna could glimpse other islanders hurrying towards the shore, heads into wind.

'Anna,' said Katrin, 'you won't believe what I'm going to tell you. I never saw the like – no, nor has anybody else in this island, I warrant.'

'An old trouble-maker,' said the voice from the bed. 'I wish she would go away.'

'What was it you saw?' said Anna.

'Come and look,' said Katrin. She took Anna by the elbow and led her outside. She pointed to the cliff.

A mast, and a piece of torn sail, stood higher than the cliff-top. The mast creaked, the sail flapped in the wind.

'What great ship can that be?' said Anna, amazed. She had certainly never seen the like of it in her eighteen years.

'A foreign ship!' said Katrin in the rapturous tones that she kept for superlative news. 'The sea threw her against the crags an hour ago. The waves are full of drowned faces. The island men are going to plunder the ship now, before she goes down. She's taking water fast. They may be too late.'

'Anna,' came the whimper from inside, 'send that mischief-maker away. I want my dinner.'

'Did none of the sailors get ashore?' cried Anna. 'God pity them all!'

'They think a few of them might have managed to get to the cave,' said Katrin. 'It doesn't matter. Hurry up, lass, if you want a share of the booty. If you're not at the cliff-top when the spoils come ashore you'll get nothing.'

And with that the news-bearer, with one last excited look at Anna, ran as fast as she could to the cliff-top, where a score of blond island-men were busy with ropes and knots.

'Father,' said Anna, 'will you be all right? I won't be long away. There's a foreign ship wrecked against the cliff – the biggest I ever saw. I'm going down to see what's happening.'

'That's right,' said her father. 'Leave me alone. Nobody knows what I'm suffering. I'm hungry too. What could *you* do at a wreck? I thought I told you a while ago to get that bride-money out of the wall. Shipwreck, indeed! That old hag and her gossip-mongering. I'll tell you what, girl – you're to go to the croft of Smelt tonight and speak to Thord Sinclair. I've sent word to him. He knows you're coming. I'm telling you, if you don't go, you'll feel the weight of my hand!' (The poor old creature, the weight of his hand would not have downed a butterfly.)

In any case, he was talking to vacancy. For Anna had taken her shawl about her and was running as fast as she could towards the cliff and the ruined mast.

When Anna got there it was too late. Great volumes of water had poured for hours through the breached hull. The first islanders were already dangling half-way down the cliff when the ship keeled over into the deep water and sank. The mast and fragment of sail (with a cross stitched on it) went in a great arc from cliff to ocean. Nothing could be seen but a vast underseas shadow.

Anna went as near to the cliff-edge as she dared and looked over. The shore was strewn with bodies.

One by one the salvagers were hauled up. The island men were bitterly disappointed. It seemed to them that such a ship must be stuffed with precious things. Now most of it would be lost in the sea. A few planks and pillows and bits of rigging – that was all they could expect.

'She was a warship,' one of the men said. 'Did you not see the row of great guns in the side of her?'

'God damn them,' said another. 'That's just what you expect of foreigners – all that splendour and show, and just when you're reaching out to grasp it, they take it from you!' (The man spoke as if the sailors had drowned their ship and themselves deliberately.)

'There's a lot of bodies down below!' cried Katrin. 'A hundred bodies if there's one! Plenty rings and bits of silk for the picking.'

That was some consolation, they all agreed. But the waves were falling in such surges at the base of the crag that they wouldn't be able to do anything about that until the wind moderated and the tide went out.

'What about the cave?' said Thord Sinclair. 'A few of them managed to scramble into the cave – I saw that with my own eyes. We could attend to them meantime.' And he took a knife out of his belt and whetted it on the palm of his hand. He turned towards the path that went down, by stone steps and ledges, to the shore.

With a shout they all, men and women, followed Thord; all except Anna, who looked uncertainly from the huge ship-shadow under the sea to the croft on the hill where her father lay.

*

The island men, a cluster of blond heads, lingered near the cave-entrance. The shawled women stood further back. Katrin's neck went this way and that like a bird.

The men hesitated. No one wanted to be the first to go in. Thord had lost much of his bravado now.

'What's wrong with you?' cried Katrin at last. 'Are you frightened of a dragon? There's nothing in there but a few half-drowned men with golden rings on their fingers.'

Still the men hung back. It was not so much cowardice or superstition; none of them wanted the blood of murder on his hands, and it might come to that once the dark spirit of avarice got into them.

Anna said, at Thord Sinclair's shoulder, 'Would you make room for me, please? There are one or two things to be done in there.' The men opened up a path for her. She passed quickly into the darkness.

How long did Anna remain in there? Some said afterwards it was a few seconds only. Some said the creature worked her shameless allurements on the young Spaniard most of the afternoon. Shame, rage, curiosity kept the islanders about the mouth of the cave. Some great mystery was being enacted inside, during which time meant nothing.

Katrin was just about to say, 'What in God's name is wrong with this island today! Do you want all the gold and silk in there to go to an ugly girl and an old done man?' She was just about to upbraid them further when Anna and a young frightened man appeared in the door of the cave. The man was carrying a dead body in his arms.

'What are you gaping at?' said Anna. 'Can't you see that this boy needs food and fire? Can't you see that his friend needs the minister and the gravedigger?'

The spell was broken. The islanders were kind merciful men in ordinary circumstances. Four of them laid gentle hands on the dead sailor. With reverence they carried him up to the church above the links. One of them went and knocked on the minister's door. Thord Sinclair went for the gravedigger.

With gentleness, inside her croft, Anna relumed the guttering flame of life in the Spaniard. The tumbling peat-flames helped; and the hot ale; and the bread and the haddocks seethed in milk and butter. Their mouths uttered an incomprehensible music, each to other – but there was more eloquence in the gestures they used to each other, in the offerings and the takings, with the elements of earth and water and fire.

All the time this mute ceremony was taking place, the voice from the box-bed sighed and moaned and raged. 'That ever I should have lived to see this! The shame of it! My lass smirking in the face of a half-dead foreigner. Putting bits of fish in his mouth. Rubbing his blue knuckles. Anna, that's my best coat – I won't have it put on his shoulders! Out he goes from this door before the sun's down. I can assure him of that. I haven't saved up all my life, and scraped and toiled, to have the dowry-money put in his hand! Never mind, Thord'll be here with a horsewhip – Thord'll see to the creature. Anna, I haven't eaten since morning. Is there a little fish in the bottom of the pot, if that black-headed beggar has quite finished? There are two beds in this house and I am in one of them. Out he goes before sunset! Does the minister know about this? I have no intention of dying, I assure you, till this is straightened out. O Lord, what will the island say about this? It's a good thing your mother's in her grave – I wish I was too. Anna, come here at once and straighten my leg!'

The slow ceremony went on all evening between the young woman and the young man. They seemed not to hear the voice from the wooden bed at all. They seemed not to be aware of the gawping face of Katrin, that lingered in the open door for as long as an egg takes to boil.

After sunset Anna lit the lamp and led the stranger to her bed. She turned back a sheet. They kissed each other. Anna blew out the flame.

The old man covered his eyes.

The croft did not wither into long spinsterhood after all. Even the foretold and longed-for death did not come knocking at that door. Before harvest Anna was married to the young Spaniard in the kirk. Together they made the croft flourish. Between them there was a proper fruitfulness also. It was the first black-haired child that restored sweetness to the mouth of the old man, after the long dark litany of sorrow; it even lured him out of his bed. One summer morning, five years later, he was still alive and hale ... There he is, sitting on the doorstep in the sunshine, with two children, the black-haired one and a younger blond one tumbling in the grass in front of him (with not a trace of Spanish in their voices). On his knee he holds an infant with black curling Spanish hair and blue Orcadian eyes. He sings to it.

Down below in the harvest field two scythes are flashing. Anna and Pedro her husband are cutting the oats. 'As for me,' says the old man to the children, 'I fell in the furrows. Thank the Lord, there are folk to finish the work.'

The scythes stop flashing. They hang suspended in the air. The old man looks. Katrin is at the edge of the field, saying something to Pedro and Anna. A stir of anger goes through the old man – that woman and her slander, the island would be well rid of her! But the two harvesters are laughing – it must be something funny and harmless, for a change.

In the next croft a harvester works in his field alone: Thord Sinclair. His scythe flames fiercely. He pays attention to no one.

Those traitorous gentlemen

In the year 1745 the laird of the island was Mr Jeremiah
Alkirk (grandson of Stephen Alkirk, whose heart had been
broken by Jennifer Jane Matilda Stoor: but not *utterly*
broken, for he got married five years later to a beautiful
English girl, Miss Penelope Jackman).

Mr Jeremiah Alkirk's factor was a man called Tom
Tweedale. Factors were, in general, feared in those times;
part of their duty was to see that the crofters and fishermen
did their work as well as they could, and paid their rents on
time, and didn't go in for smuggling and witchcraft – activi-
ties damaging to state and religion as by law established.
This Mr Tom Tweedale was the most indulgent factor the

islanders had known. He never harried them or bullied them. They felt he was one of themselves rather than an instrument of authority. Indeed, his words and actions were clean contrary to his position as the laird's chief man. He would say to the kelp-gatherers on the shore, in his black voice, 'This isn't right at all! It's against nature! All this seaweed should be yours. The day is coming. This island should belong to you and to you alone. If you had any guts you could take over the crofts and the fishing boats this same day! You're a poor lot, right enough!'

The islanders didn't know what to make of the man. Was he trying to get them into trouble? Suppose one or two of the younger men were to throw down their forks and shout, 'You're right, brother Tweedale! Be our leader! Attention, everybody – the island belongs to us – Tweedale is to lead us to the laird's door this same morning – now!' The young fools would be arrested on the spot and sent on to Kirkwall prison in chains; so the old men and women whispered to each other behind their hands. To some of the islanders it seemed that Tom Tweedale was more than an *agent provocateur* – what he urged was perilously close to blasphemy and treason.

Sometimes on a Sunday afternoon when they were all trooping kirkwards, there was the powerful morose creature leaning on the kirkyard wall smoking a pipe. 'Have you nothing better to do,' he would shout, 'than sit on a fine day listening to that old drone with his fire and brimstone? Look at the free clouds up there. Look at the sun and the huge blue sea. They're God's handiworks, and He wants us to enjoy them. That's what I'm going to do anyway – I'll worship out here in "greenfields kirk".'

The crofters and their wives, all dressed in sober black, would cringe away from that dreadful impious voice. They would turn their heads away deliberately, and go doucely, with clasped hands, in through the open door of the kirk.

Nobody could understand why the laird kept this subversive man in his service. Once the minister had gone to the Hall (the laird's big house) and complained. 'Really, Mr Alkirk, the time has come for something to be done. That factor is undermining both your authority and mine. He is sowing unrest in their minds. Of course the people in general are sound – they turn a deaf ear to all that dangerous nonsense of his. But one or two of the young men have caught the infection. "This is *our* island," they say, pointing to the hill and the shore. The poor creatures, they believe it. I lay the blame entirely at the door of your Mr Tweedale.'

'Tom Tweedale,' said the laird, 'is a good man. He loves the whole human race. I wish there were more folk like him in the world.'

The minister seemed to take that remark as a personal rebuke. 'Very well, sir,' he shouted. 'If you don't do something about the man, there are others that will.'

'Good-day to you, minister,' said Mr Alkirk sweetly.

And the minister went, red in the face, and banged the huge door after him till the timbers rattled.

Tom Tweedale was riding round the island one day in the summer of 1745 when his attention was drawn by three tiny gesticulating figures on the shore of Selskay island across the Sound. What on earth were they signalling – distress or triumph?

The factor raised his glass to his eye. Three magnified dandies swam into the lens, and were merrily imprisoned there. The viewer recognized all three of them: Mr Blount the laird of Selskay, and Mr Jaffray the laird of Norday, and Mr Wynne-Friel the episcopal minister from Kirkwall.

'Grinders of the poor,' said Tom Tweedale to his horse. 'They're up to something. It looks to me there wouldn't take much to set them dancing. All dressed up to the nines, too! What's afoot?'

He called down to a fisherman who was caulking a boat among the rocks. 'Josie,' he yelled. 'Leave the tarpot. Take that other boat and row across for those gentlemen. It seems they have business with our gentleman.'

Josie pushed out the boat. The factor turned his horse round and urged it on towards the Hall. 'Your peers are wanting to see you,' he said brusquely to Mr Alkirk. 'They're on the way now. It looks to me as if they've been having a drink already.'

The news that Mr Blount, Mr Jaffray, and Mr Wynne-Friel brought to the island that day was that Prince Charles Edward Stuart had landed from a French ship on the west coast of Scotland. There the clans had quickly rallied to the handsome gay young prince. The kilted army, ever growing in numbers, had marched south-east towards Edinburgh, the Scottish capital. They had met an army of the up-start King George, led by Sir John Cope, and had utterly routed it. The true prince had entered the capital in triumph.

Never had there been such joy in the Hall, for wedding, baptism, or jubilee. The lady of the Hall kissed the three news-bearers one after the other. A keg of the best brandy was taken up from the cellar, and half-a-dozen ringing loyal Stuart toasts were drunk.

Into the midst of this revelry came the minister, drawn by curiosity. 'My dear man,' said the laird, 'come over here to the fire! Penelope, see that Mr MacIsaac's glass is charged. Mr MacIsaac, this is the greatest news since the pirate Gow was captured in Eday – oh far, far greater! I have waited all my life for this day. If only my poor father knew, he would clap his hands in his coffin.'

The minister was much put out to see Mr Wynne-Friel there – presbyterians and episcopalians had small truck with each other in those days. All the same he raised the goblet to his lips. What windfall could have happened to set the great ones of Orkney in such a bleeze of joy – a school of whales ashore on Selskay? a French privateer captured, freighted with doubloons and escudos?

'Drink, my dear MacIsaac,' said the laird, 'to our true sovereign, King James the Third, and to his gallant and victorious son the prince Charles Edward!'

The minister put down his goblet, highly offended. 'I am a loyal subject of King George,' he said. 'I will have no part in treason. I ask you, gentlemen, to think well of what you're doing.'

On the road outside, he could hear the laughter of the gentlemen; and then the pledging of yet another traitorous toast. And then ivory-shouldered Mrs Alkirk began to play on the clavichord.

The islanders, gathered that night in the alehouse, were eager to know what the great ones were celebrating. Could it be that Mistress Blount over in Selskay had given birth at last to an heir? Maybe war had been declared against France or Denmark – in that case they would have to keep wary eyes open for the press-gang; they would have to see to the provisioning of the caves . . .

Into the tobacco-haze and the speculation Mr Tweedale wandered. Would the landlord be kind enough to pour him a gill of malt?

'War,' he said to the drinkers. 'It's civil war. Those Stuarts have come over the seas from France again and upset the applecart. You never saw such sights as up in the Hall this day! Dancing, singing, drinking of brandy. All foolishness. But I bring you good news, men.'

They crowded about him.

'Your next half-yearly rents are remitted, in honour of this day.'

The island men raised their tankards and cheered. 'Long live the Stuart king!' one of them shouted; and there were great gulpings and wiping of frothy moustaches.

'That's all the good it'll do you,' said Mr Tweedale. 'No matter who wins this war, Stuart or Hanoverian, you'll still have to drudge in the furrows like oxen till you die.'

But the island men were too excited at the news to be affected by that gloomy man and his dark words. The barrel was broached and tapped again until it gurgled and expired.

'As for the gentlemen of Orkney,' said the factor – 'the Lord help them if the dice fall the wrong way!'

Scraps of news about the war filtered into the island from time to time, brought by travellers or skippers or tinkers. The laird heard the latest information first of all, of course. In Edinburgh the victorious prince had held great triumphs and balls. The ladies of Scotland one and all had lost their hearts to him. But there was serious business yet to be done ... The prince was marching south (came the intelligence) at the head of his army. The numerous Jacobites of the north of England would fall over themselves to join him. In London there was great panic. The Hanoverian gentry had stowed all their plate and coin into chests ready for shipment to Germany or Holland. The king himself – that upstart who could only speak broken English – was about to look on Windsor and Whitehall for the last time ...

The prince had reached Derby; he was pausing there to re-group, replenish, before marching swiftly and irresistibly on London ... The laird told the islanders that news one day in the harvest-field. They had never known him so merry. 'God bless you, Andrew,' he said to the oldest harvester, and put his arm about him – 'this is a sweet time to be alive in!'

'For lairds, not for crofters,' muttered Tom Tweedale among the stooks . . .

After that there was no news for a month or two. Any day the laird expected to hear of the fall of London. He had promised the island a celebration – free ale and meat and music in the garden of the Hall. He had even imported a box of fireworks from Aberdeen.

A skipper who was sheltering at Hamnavoe was taken to the laird's door just after New Year. The laird welcomed the man with open arms. (He had given orders that all merchant skippers should be invited to the island, whether they had news or not.)

'One thing is certain,' said this skipper, 'the rebels haven't taken London. I sailed out of Gravesend a week ago. I'm bound for Sweden with a cargo of wool. The city was in a great panic a month ago – you never saw such running here and there, and bribings, and booking of passages. But now everything's back to normal. The worst is past. There's no danger now, they say. God save good King George.'

'But are you sure of this?' asked the laird.

The skipper nodded. He had an honest face.

'Now,' said the laird after a pause, 'have you heard anything about the prince and his army?'

'In full retreat,' said the skipper. 'The savages, with their naked legs and heads like haystacks! The king's son, Cumberland, is after them in full cry. I heard the pretender is back in Scotland.'

'Well, I thank you,' said the laird, and put half-a-sovereign in his visitor's hand; and the skipper had not heard a voice that, in the course of half-an-hour, so changed from silvery hope to the lead of despondency.

It was an old tinker, five months later, that brought the last chapter of the story to the Hall. 'A more fearful and pitiful sight I never seen,' she said. 'The moor of Drumossie strewn with the dead and the dying. And there the red-coats going from body to body like vultures, taking the eagle feathers from their bonnets and the little crucifixes from round their necks. Sir, if they saw a spark of life they put it out at once – dagger into throat. I never saw such cruelty. Ah, sir, courtesy and kindness is gone now from the glens for ever!'

'Come in, Madge,' said the laird. 'It's a cold afternoon. You'll take a glass of whisky with me. God bless you, Madge.' (It was the first time laird and tinker had ever drunk together.)

'Now,' he said, when the rims of their glasses were still ringing from a dark pledge, 'the prince. Have you heard, Madge, how it has gone with him?'

'In the west,' said the old woman. 'They're after him in full cry, thousands of red-coats. The government has offered a great fortune to them that will betray him – thirty thousand pounds. Sir, I didn't know there was that much money in the world! I saw him myself in the heather one day with the few friends he has left. He was as merry as a boy flying a kite. I said to myself that day, "Madge, off with you to the garrison at Fort William – you're finished with gnawing on bones and roots – you're the richest woman in Scotland!" Then I said to myself again, "Madge, you have a soul to save. Madge, you are the sister of all hunted and harried ones – the trout and the otter and the man escaping from the law." So I sat on my bum inside my tent till the darling one was out of sight in the mist. Next day I came north to the islands.'

'God bless you, Madge,' said the laird, and filled her glass again, and wept.

'Tom,' said the alehouse keeper to the factor one summer evening that same year as they sat at the open alehouse door smoking their pipes, 'I haven't seen Mr Alkirk for days and days. Must be a fortnight. I hope he isn't ill?'

'The man of the Hall,' said Tom Tweedale, 'has been called away on business. And I'd be very much obliged if *you* would mind *your* business, the serving of ale. My mug has been empty for half an hour, man.'

Next day the whole island knew why Mr Alkirk had gone away so suddenly. A company of sailors led by a lieutenant arrived in the island from Selskay. They had rowed over in a longboat. A crowd of islanders gathered quickly at the landing-place. The lieutenant shouted, 'There's a man in this island by the name of Alkirk – I want to know where he is!'

The islanders weren't used to such hectoring. Not a man spoke.

'You, man,' cried the officer, and took Josie Tarbreck by the elbow. 'You know where he must be!'

Josie Tarbreck shook his head.

'So,' said the lieutenant – 'an island of traitors! Do you know this, you could all be jailed, maybe hanged, for rebelling against King George! I advise you to cooperate with me.'

The minister came down the shore path from the fields above. 'Good day to you, sir,' he said to the lieutenant. 'I'm the island minister, and as good a subject of King George as you are, sir. These people here are simple and honest. They scarcely know what king is on the throne. It's all one to them. Now, sir, can I help you?'

The lieutenant demanded once more to know where the laird was.

'This is the truth, sir,' said the minister. 'The laird left his house a full fortnight ago. Neither his wife nor his children know where he is.'

The officer nodded. 'That makes nine of them. Nine traitors in high places here in Orkney, and all of them vanished! We have just been in Selskay looking for Mr Blount. He wasn't at home either. The only notable traitor we have secured is the parson in Kirkwall. He will have plenty of leisure in the prison-hulk to say his prayers.'

'Traitor or no, sir,' said the minister, '(and he and I, sir, did not agree in matters of politics) Mr Alkirk was a good landlord to his people.'

There was a nodding of heads, murmurs of agreement, all along the shore.

'They will be found and punished, those traitorous gentlemen,' said the lieutenant. 'Depend upon it. Meantime it is our duty to search the house.'

In the Hall they were received by Mrs Alkirk. There was a pallor in her beauty those days. 'Look where you wish,' she said. 'My husband is not here. Mr Tweedale the factor is at your service.'

Tom Tweedale showed them every room and possible hiding-place from attic to cellar. The lieutenant knocked on a parlour wall and a hollow echo came back. 'Aha!' he said, and raised his eyebrows. Without a word Tom Tweedale ripped three varnished planks out. Inside there was a community of spiders in their intricate airy houses. 'There was no need to go to such an extent,' said the lieutenant.

'I am entirely at your service,' said Tom Tweedale.

The officer and his men returned to their longboat without Mr Jeremiah Alkirk.

Sometimes, in the kirk on a Sunday, the minister would read out one or two announcements – it might be from the sheriff in Kirkwall, or the chief excise officer, or the feudal authorities in Edinburgh. On this particular Sabbath afternoon the announcement came from the factor. 'The man never darkens the door of this kirk,' said the minister grimly. 'In fact he encourages you in atheism – I've heard him at it. Yet he expects me to read out to you, from this holy pulpit, his directives. We are bidden in scripture to be charitable. Dig the wax out of your ears then, brethren, and listen: "Prohibited Territory – Until further notice that shore known as the Bay of Seals is out of bounds to all islanders and visitors to this island, without exception. Any man or woman found trespassing there will be severely dealt with. By order of me, the factor of the estate, Thomas MacAlpine Tweedale." '

'I have my boat there!' cried Josie Tarbreck from a pew in the middle of the kirk where he sat with his wife and eight bairns and his dog Hussie.

'Listen, my friend,' said the minister, 'nobody lifts his voice in this kirk, except in the psalm-singing, but me the minister. In such a secular business you will deal with Mr Tweedale in a place and on a day suitable for such business.'

In the end Josie had to remove his fishing boat to another beach.

The islanders wondered very much as to why the Bay of Seals had been made prohibited territory. Some thought Tweedale was going in for a little private smuggling. Others were of opinion that he intended, now that he was practically the master of the island, to do a trade in sealskins. 'It's just this,' said Robert the blacksmith, 'he's a very awkward man by nature. He likes to make difficulties.'

'Where's the equality now that he's always shouting about?' said Willie the weaver.

The people kept their eyes on Tom Tweedale. The man had become exceedingly abrupt and disobliging. That something strange was afoot at the Bay of Seals was obvious to everybody. The factor was there very often; especially at morning twilight and evening twilight they would see the sombre bulk of him against the sky, in the fields above the bay, coming or going, and sometimes with a burden on his shoulder.

There was one crofter called Peter Aith. He was an easy-going man himself, but his wife was very inquisitive – her eyes went here and there, her sharp tongue probed every action and every situation. It must have been her that nagged and bullied her man into the forbidden territory.

Peter Aith, looking cautiously from a coign of the cliff one sunset, saw nothing out of the way in the Bay of Seals at all – no mermaids, no foreigners with bales of silk on their shoulders, no oyster-shells with the pearls gouged out. His wife had suggested all these possibilities.

'Well, sir,' said a black voice, 'and would you be taking a constitutional before your supper?'

'Just that,' said Peter Aith, too overcome for apology or lies. He looked round. There, towering above him, stood Tweedale the factor.

'I thought I had told you, man, and everybody else, to keep away from here,' said Tweedale in his low dangerous voice. 'Why have you disobeyed me?'

Peter Aith was not a coward. 'What right have you,' he cried, 'to forbid us this beach? The laird never kept us from coming here! The beach is free territory. The men of this island have always had the right to take seaweed and sand from the Bay of Seals.'

Tom Tweedale lifted Peter Aith by the scruff of the neck and the waistband of his breeches and carried him, kicking and raging, up the steep path and across the cornfield and pasture; and finally he threw him in at the open door of his croft.

'Have a care of your man,' he said to the fluttering croft-wife. 'Hide his boots next time he feels like a dander. For if you don't, ma'am, there's such a thing, I promise you, as eviction.'

The whole island laughed next day when the news got about. But there was uneasiness in the mirth at smithy and ale-house. Tweedale could be a terrible man in his rages. No islander thereafter walked on that beach while the prohibition remained in force.

Poor Peter Aith was so ashamed of himself that he never showed his face for a week. As for Mistress Aith, she whispered darkly to Mistress Tarbreck one morning when they were at the well getting water, 'I believe, Willumina, if the sand was to be dug there, they would find the murdered corpse of Mr Alkirk, with a red wound on him.'

Mistress Tarbreck told her for mercy's sake not to whisper such a thing. She might find herself in great trouble. 'As for that good man the laird, wherever he is, the Lord look to him.'

The following spring an official edict of clemency was issued. It stated that certain proscribed persons who had shown sympathy for the late rebellion in His Majesty's domains were now to be pardoned because they had played no active part in the traitorous uprising, either by bearing arms themselves or by supplying men or arms or money on behoof of the pretender to the throne and his French-subsidized son.

That edict was read out one cold Sunday afternoon in the kirk.

The next day the mystery of the Bay of Seals was explained. Out of the cave Tom Tweedale led half-a-dozen pitiable-looking scarecrows. A few of them were tottery on their legs; the factor had to carry them on to the road above. One of them sat on the wall and wept for joy.

The islanders did not recognize their master. He was emaciated; he had a cough that racked his whole body; one of his arms seemed to hang useless. It was only when Mrs Alkirk threw herself at him and fell weeping on his limpet-smelling shoulder that they were sure.

By evening the last of the Jacobite gentlemen had left the island for their own homes; distinctly more pleasant dwellings than the hole in the rock that had sheltered them all winter.

They would all certainly have died – they let it be known – but for the ministrations of Tom Tweedale. Twice a day, under the morning or the evening star, he had brought food and clothes, and the latest news to them. In fact one of the lairds had died before Christmas, an old haughty man. 'If I get out of here, ever,' he had said, 'I'll see well to the poorest of my tenants.' ... Tweedale had to bury him on the foreshore. (Mistress Aith, the gossip, was right to the extent that there was a body under the sand.)

'Did you have a good look at them when they came out of the cave?' said Tom Tweedale that same night in the alehouse. 'Was there ever such a bunch of scarecrows in the land? Did you ever see tramp or tinker that looked more wretched? That, brothers, is your landlord without benefit of silk or scent. He holds your lives in the hollow of his hand. Time an end was put to it. It will come all right.'

'Can I beach my boat on that shore again?' asked Josie Tarbreck.

'To be sure, man,' said the factor. 'The ban is lifted. As for you, Peter Aith, I owe you an apology for the way I carted you from the beach that evening. It had to be done. Landlord, give Peter Aith a glass of malt, and charge me.'

Smugglers

The beaches and rocks on the west of the islands were Forg's hunting ground. It was a rare day that something didn't come ashore – a piece of timber, or a barrel, or an old boot. Most of what Forg picked out of the ebb had no value. All the same he would hold a sea-warped boot in his hand and look at it with wonderment. Who had worn it? Had it been a happy man or a melancholy man? Rich or poor? Married or (like Forg himself) a careless bachelor? What dust had this boot stirred? How came it in the sea? – perhaps the man had gone down to wash his feet in a pool and a great wave had come crashing in and carried his boots off swirling into deep water. Then the man would have to walk home on bare feet, and what a talking-to he would get from his wife! Forg laughed at the thought of it. Perhaps a ship's officer had worn it, who had been thrown into the sea by mutineers. Forg's cheeks blanched at the terror of that death.

Many things far more amazing than an old boot Forg found on the western shore. Once he had come on a box of yellow balls. They were heavy and oily. The sea had saturated them to the core. He brought one or two to the minister, and displayed them, after touching his cap obsequiously. 'Oranges,' said the minister. 'Good for the chest. The sea's been at 'em, Forg. You couldn't eat 'em now. They must be from that Spanish ship that wrecked on the Fair Isle.' ... 'Thank you, sir,' said Forg humbly, 'for telling me.' Back at the rock, he ate one of the oranges, and was sick into a pool. 'I suppose,' said Forg, 'only foreigners could eat such stuff.'

Once Forg saw a basket with a graceful glass neck dandling in the waves, uncertain whether to come ashore or to give itself to the tide-race. Forg helped it to make up its mind. The contents of that basket gave him two blissfully happy days, but for the rest of the week he had to endure a dreadful hangover. 'Still, it was worth it,' said Forg. He searched the whole coastline thoroughly for more flagons, but without success.

Once he turned a swathe of seaweed and a beautiful dead face looked up at him. He put one tremulous kiss on the cheek – it was the only girl he had ever been allowed to kiss in his life – and then turned and ran in terror to tell the factor. The unknown girl was buried in the kirkyard that same afternoon.

Sometimes there would be a shipwreck on the island. That was altogether too much for Forg. The matter was taken out of his hands – he was swept aside by the plunderers. Officially all wrecks belonged to the king, but by the time the king's representatives got to the scene the ship had been picked clean. 'Ah, sir,' a crofter would say to the laird, 'the ship's bare as a skeleton. She must have been abandoned in mid-Atlantic six months or more ago! . . .' But Forg, out of bad temper and jealousy and rage, would whisper to the factor (the laird's overseer), 'That ship was fully freighted when she struck. Look into their barns. Look in the smithy. Look in the vestry of the kirk – I saw the beadle going up with his shoulder burdened.'

It will be seen that Forg did not consider himself to be one of the peasants. He was a solitary, a man apart. He was poorer than anybody in the island, yet he had the ear of factor and minister. Forg told them things about island on-goings (love, illicit drinking, kirk avoidance, peat stealing) that he thought they ought to know. Many a silver coin passed between the hands of authority and the cringing hand of Forg.

Forg's harvest-time, which might occur seven or eight times in a year, fell after a severe westerly gale. Then, with luck, the entire western shore would be piled with debris; and Forg would be up at first light, to toil like a galley slave among the rubbish till the sun went down. Rubbish it was mostly, but each object touched the imagination of the beachcomber. And sometimes he might find something valuable. The previous month the carpenter in Kirkwall had given him a pound for a beam of timber.

Times were bad for Forg one autumn. For more than a month the island had been blessed with an Indian summer. Mellow autumn light fell across the shorn fields. The crofters let their beasts roam free still – while this weather lasted it would be wrong to shut them in their dark winter prisons. The sea moved serenely against the shore, like a lover, with kissings and songs.

'Devil take it,' said Forg on the shore. 'Why can't it blow?

It's the time of the year for storms!' He found an empty bottle, and smashed it against the rocks.

After twenty fruitless days – during which time he had to depend on the random charity of croft-wives, and a sixpence from the minister for whispering to him that Rob of Mossgar was in love with Freda of Waithe – Forg decided to shift his ground. He would comb the Bay of Seals.

Forg didn't like that particular stretch of coast. For one thing, it was in the north-west of the island, and so didn't trap the main sea-borne treasure drift. Also he didn't like seals, with their great soul-piercing eyes. If he had had the courage he wouldn't have minded clubbing a few of them: the flesh of them made a rich if indigestible stew, and he knew a shopkeeper in Kirkwall who was prepared to buy sealskin . . . Most of all he was afraid of the cave.

Hunger makes a man do things that he doesn't particularly care to do. One evening, late, Forg found himself at the Bay of Seals, poking and probing among the pools and the strewn seaweed. It was a quiet evening. The first star glittered in a rockpool. Forg found a salt-eaten boot.

It was just then that Forg was aware of voices at the far end of the bay, where the cave was. He could not make out any words, only the mingled music of a dialogue. There was excitement in it, and warning, and daring. Then the urgent whisperers must have climbed up on to the links above. Forg saw, against the crimson skyline, two figures with burdened shoulders. They were too far away for Forg to recognize. One of them limped a bit – that must be Magnus of Noust. The two furtive shadows were lost soon in the solid shadow of the hill.

'What's this?' said Forg. 'There's been no shipwreck since February. I smell crime and I smell felony.' He decided that it was too early yet to say anything to the factor. He needed more evidence. If it hadn't been so late and so dark he would have had a peek into the cave. The whisperers, the burdened shadows, seemed to have some connection with the cave, that dreadful place. Forg decided to keep his ears and eyes open.

Next morning, as soon as the sun got up, Forg was out of his hut breakfastless and down with him to the Bay of Seals. There was not a soul stirring in the island; only the animals moved at peace in their pastures, cherishing the freedom of one more beautiful autumn day.

Across the rocks Forg clambered, ignoring bottles that winked at him and boots that gaped at him. Once he stumbled on seaweed and pain seared from his elbow to his shoulder like a stroke of lightning. His arm hung useless for an hour. Forg considered that it was wiser, all the same, to come this perilous way than to leave footprints in the sand.

At last he arrived at the cave mouth. Forg was not a man who rushed into delights or danger. He hung about a rock-pool for a time, piercing through the glassy surface with an expert eye. There were half-a-hundred whelks in the pool. The minister's sister liked whelks for her supper, with a cup of porter. He would call with them at the Manse door, price one penny.

'What are you seeking here?' said a voice.

Forg nearly died on the spot. He knew the voice – it belonged to Alec of Sholt, a man who had never showed much kindness to Forg in the past. There wasn't any sweetness in his voice this morning either.

'I'm looking for whelks,' said Forg.

'I didn't think, Forg man,' said Alec of Sholt, 'that this was your hunting-ground at all. Would you not be better further west? This is a dangerous place, man, a very unchancy place.'

'I have as much right here as you have,' said Forg. 'Leave me alone.'

'Forg, man,' said Alec of Sholt, 'there's something about you that I do not like. There's a shiftiness about you. You're as cunning and as dangerous as a rat. I have a scunner at you, Forg. I do not like to be in the same place with you. Be off with you now.'

'The beach doesn't belong to you,' said Forg. 'It belongs to the laird, down to low-water mark. I have the laird's permission to comb any island beach I choose.'

'I've heard tell,' said Alec of Sholt, 'and I believe it, that in exchange for the laird's bounty you pass certain information on to him. And generally this information bodes no good for us poor crofters at all.'

'What I do and what I don't do is my own business,' said Forg.

'Forg,' said Alec of Sholt, 'you will oblige me by leaving this beach at once.'

'I intend to be here,' said Forg, 'all this week, maybe longer.'

At that, the crofter leapt at the beachcomber and took him by the scruff of the neck and began to drag him away from the cave mouth. Forg lashed out with his foot and kicked Alec on the kneecap. Alec yelled and struck Forg with his fist on the mouth. Forg yelped. Alec struck him again and he staggered and fell among the seaweed.

Forg raised himself on his fists and knees and looked wildly about for some means of escape. It would be no easy thing to win clear of this lithe brutal man. He heard a mild voice saying, 'What on earth is all this about? You can be heard for miles. Do you want the whole world flocking to this cave? Two grown men. I'm surprised at you, Alec.'

Forg saw, without surprise, that the speaker was Magnus of Noust, the crofter who had one leg shorter by two inches than the other. Magnus was a gentle good-natured man.

Forg liked him – he had given Forg bread and ale many a winter night at his fire.

'We'll have no more of this nonsense,' said Magnus. 'Get on your feet, Forg. Unclench your fists, Alec. The fight's over.'

The great brute from the croft of Sholt looked ashamed of himself now, lounging against the sandstone buttress of the cliff. Mercifully, Magnus had a good influence over him.

'It was him that started it,' said Forg, nodding darkly at Alec.

'And *I'm* going to finish it,' said Magnus, smiling. 'Now, Forg, there's nothing on this beach for you – nothing at all. Wouldn't you be better somewhere else?'

'I can go where I like, Magnus,' muttered Forg.

'Of course you can,' said Magnus. 'Look, man, I'm sorry this has happened. Alec's sorry too, but he's too stubborn to say so. Pride in a man is a terrible thing.'

Magnus opened his fist and showed Forg a silver four-penny piece. 'This is for you, Forg,' he said. 'Compensation.'

The fact that a poor crofter had so much money to squander was an added matter of suspicion to Forg. He lifted the silver coin from Magnus's palm. 'He's split my lip,' he said. 'It's bleeding.'

'Dear me,' said Magnus, 'so it is, Forg. Alec, you're a very violent man. Never do such a thing again to Forg, my friend. I know you're too obstinate to ask Forg's pardon, in so many words. See if you can show your sorrow in some other way.'

Alec, for all his mulishness, seemed to understand. He rummaged in his breeches pocket and dredged up a handful of coins – Forg had never known a crofter to possess such wealth – and, having selected a shilling, put it into Forg's hand without a word.

'Now, Forg,' said Magnus, 'just to make sure that you and Alec don't fall afighting again, I'm going to ask you a favour. Don't come combing about in this bay for the next month. Alec and I will be here a lot of the time. It's the seals. Alec and I have this arrangement with Mr Fleming, the merchant in Kirkwall, for an urgent supply of sealskins.'

With these words he opened his fist again, and a silver sixpence passed between Magnus and Forg. Even while he was accepting, thanklessly, the bounty, Forg was thinking to himself, 'The liar that he is! Magnus is too gentle a man to take the life of a seal. Besides, it isn't the time of year for seal-hunting.'

Forg touched his cap and turned to go. 'He hasn't promised,' said Alec sullenly.

Forg would promise anybody the kingdom of heaven. Promises to him were as random as snowflakes or butterflies. 'I promise,' he said with dignity. 'I will leave you to your seal-hunting for the next month. But it must be understood that I, Forg, have as much right to be on this beach as anybody else – more right, for beachcombing is my trade. But you have my promise.'

'Good man, Forg,' said Magnus.

The picture began to piece itself together in Forg's mind as this last day of the Indian summer passed. There had been that French ship anchored off the headland for two nights in the dark of the last moon. Of course the excise officers had boarded her; but French ship-builders were cunning with their concealed holds and double hulls.

Forg decided to waste no time. He was certain of a handsome reward. It was not the first time he had passed on information to the excise.

That evening – though he was not a drinking man – he looked into the alehouse at the crossroads. There in the company, among swirls of pipe smoke and tilted pewter, sat Magnus of Noust and Alec of Sholt. Forg asked at the counter for a schooner of ale. 'Mercy,' cried the landlord, 'what's happened to your mouth, Forg? Have you been in a fight?'

'A dog bit me on the shore,' said Forg, 'an ignorant brute of a hound that should have been done away with at birth.'

Alec of Sholt drew his brows together, but Magnus, sitting beside the fire, smiled and nodded at Forg.

Forg drank his ale down quickly and went out.

In the depths of the cave Forg found, by the light of a tallow candle, a vast hoard – twenty kegs of brandy, fifty cones of tobacco bound with tarred string, five barrels of sugar, besides many boxes and chests whose contents he could only guess at. It was enough. He went straight from the cave to the factor's house on the side of the hill.

'I should think,' said Mr Mackenzie, 'this information would be worth ten guineas to you, Forg. No need for you to get rheumatics and coughs beachcombing this winter, Forg.'

The excise officers came secretly to the island two nights later. They had a dozen hired strong-arm men with them from Kirkwall. They played cards in the factor's parlour all night. They entered the cave at dawn next morning. Behind a barrel they discovered Magnus of Noust. Magnus gave himself up at once, smiling. 'I take no offence,' he said. 'I broke the law. I must be punished. That's the way things go.'

Behind another barrel there was sudden violence. Alec struggled like a bull in the hands of the excise assistants. He raged against them. 'Bring ropes,' cried an exciseman. 'This is a mad beast.'

'Now Alec,' said Magnus, 'you're making it worse for yourself.'

Alec managed to tear himself out of the hands that were holding him. He reached into a niche of the cave wall. The cave was suddenly all flame and smoke. When the pandemonium died, it was discovered that an exciseman was lying against the wall of the cave with blood on his hands and coat. The pistol ball had entered his throat. He coughed and retched for ten minutes, then died without a word.

The two island crofters were hanged in Kirkwall a month later, for murder. Only one of them had fired the shot, but both had been engaged in the felony, and so were judged equally guilty.

Forg did not outlive them long. Before Christmas he was found dead on the beach. 'Ah,' cried the old women, 'the cold must have seized his heart. He didn't eat enough fish and soup. He was a poor shadow of a creature all his days. Well, he won't be much of a miss, that Forg – a sleazy thing!'

But the old women were wrong, for once. Forg's body was completely shattered. It was obvious to the factor and the minister that he had fallen, or been thrown, from a height. They tilted their faces at the summit of the crag, which was two hundred and thirty feet high at this point. It was unlikely to have been an accident; Forg was sure-footed as a goat.

'It is useless, I think,' said the factor, 'to look for a murderer. Two hangings in one island is enough for this generation, anyway. It is more a purification than a murder. There was a boil in the life of the island, and the island has lanced it. I must look for another informer. That will not be easy. Forg was good at the job.'

Forg the beachcomber lies nameless among the lettered stonefast dead in the island kirkyard.

The feast of the strangers

When the days got very dark, in the middle of winter, the woman who lived in the croft down at the shore was never happy till her three sons were home and the door was shut for the night. Then the lamp was lit and the peatfire blown into flame. They ate their supper and were in bed long before midnight.

The woman had reason to fear winter. The previous January her husband and two neighbours had gone fishing. A sudden storm came out of the north. The boat had never returned.

By good fortune her eldest boy Peter had newly learned to handle a boat and to fish with his father. Now Peter was the breadwinner. Yet she dreaded that the sea might take him too, some day.

The second boy, Sam, was the joy of her heart. He knew everybody in the island; he was welcome at nearly every door. Even the laird's sour-faced sister would take Sam in from his wanderings about the roads and give him gingerbread and cinnamon water. He would come back to the croft after a long day and tell his mother and brothers all the news he had heard. He told the stories so drolly, and with such fine mimicry of the island voices, that they had to laugh. Even Gib laughed. Sam, the mother knew, would be a good ploughman, a good provider, in a year or two.

Gib was the youngest boy. The less said about him the better. The island folk said of Gib that he was 'trowie' – that is, the trows (or trolls) must have stolen the true child and left Gib – one of their own offspring – in the cradle instead. All he was allowed to do was feed the beasts. Some nights he slept in the byre himself.

'Now,' said the minister in the kirk one Sunday, 'it's getting on for Yule, the very darkest time of the year. But this is the time that the Lord of All chose to give us men a very precious gift, his own Son.' . . . Then he read to them out of his big black bible the story of the Nativity, which of course they knew by heart already. 'We must be thinking,' said he, 'of some way of showing our gratitude for that gift. We should put ourselves in the place of those three kings who came to the village where the Child was, bringing gifts. Let us seriously think of the gifts we can bring to the church next Friday and the days following.' . . .

The days dwindled and darkened down to the solstice, but remained calm, so that Peter was able to go fishing every day. On the Thursday Gib said to Peter, 'Peter, I want to come out in the boat with you, to catch a few fish.' . . . 'You will *not*,' said the mother sharply. 'A boat is dangerous enough without a clumsy creature like you in it.'

Gib said, 'All right then, Mother.'

Gib wandered away to a neighbouring farm, where a bad-tempered man called Jacob Taing lived.

'Mr Taing,' said Gib, 'do you remember when I helped in your oatfield at harvest? You forgot to pay me a wage.'

'You – a wage!' said Jacob Taing. 'You were a hindrance to everybody! You got in the way of the scythes. Away home with you.'

But Mrs Taing took Gib into the house. She brought a barley scone out of the cupboard, cut it in five pieces, and wrapped the portions up.

'There's your harvest wages, Gib,' she said. 'A good Yule to you, when it comes.'

Gib went home with his bread.

When Peter returned before sunset, Gib was standing on the shore. Peter set down a box of fish on the rock. He gave two haddocks to Gib. 'That's for you, Gib,' he said. 'The fish you wanted. I'm back from the west just in time. There's a storm breeding in the north – look!' . . . There was a blue-black bruise indeed on the northern horizon.

Gib laid his two haddocks in a rockpool; then he followed Peter up to the croft, a hundred slow steps behind.

Sam came back, red-cheeked, from the heart of the island, just after sunset when there was a jet-and-scarlet smoulder in the west. He could hardly wait to tell them the news. 'There's wandering folk in the island,' he said. 'Strangers. I didn't see them myself. They're among the hills. They're living in an old patched tent. The factor's on the lookout with his dog and gun – he's going to clear them out. They have no business in the island at all . . .'

After supper, while they were sitting round the fire, the mother said, 'Tomorrow's Yule. I have a shilling put by for the kirk. It took me all winter to save up the ha'pennies and pennies. You, Peter, will have to give something too.'

Peter said he had a sixpenny piece put by, ever since the big haul of lobsters in summer.

Sam, tired out, was sleeping in the chair.

Gib asked his mother if she remembered how he had helped her on the peat-hill the summer before. The mother said, 'You got in everybody's way! You fell in a peat-bank and you were as black as Satan, and half-drowned, when I dragged you out!'

'I want three peats for my day's wages,' said Gib.

Sam woke up and immediately remembered about the dark strangers. 'Everybody's frightened,' he said. 'Every croft's going to bar its door tonight.'

'I will too,' said the mother. 'I'll bar this door.'

'The good weather's at an end,' said Peter. 'I won't get to the fishing this side of Hogmanay. God help any poor folk with no roof over their heads!'

Even as he spoke, the first gust struck the end of the croft house. The door shook. The smoke wavered in the hearth.

Gib said he wouldn't go to bed yet. He would sit at the dark window and watch the storm outside for a while. All he needed was a candle on the window-ledge.

'You'll do no such thing!' cried his mother. 'You'll go to your bed at once like the rest of us! What an idea. This is the night, Christmas Eve, that the trows are out in their thousands – black hordes of them! Every Christian body must be abed.'

But she knew that Gib would do exactly what he said. The boy's nature was a weave of sweetness and obstinacy.

'Say the good words,' said the mother to Peter, sighing.

Peter held up his hand. He chanted 'the good words' – 'Lord, look on this croft in mercy and pity. Make us thankful for our fire and food and shelter. May a kind angel guard this island this night. Amen.'

Peter and Sam went to bed then. The woman of the house dimmed the flame of the lamp. Gib crouched in the window-seat with his candle-flame, looking beyond the washed and shuddering pane, into darkness. His mother barred the door.

There was a lamentation of storm over the island all that night. Old folk couldn't sleep for the noises of wind and sea.

In the first light of morning, when Peter looked out, the Sound was all grey and black and white. The window-seat was empty. Gib must have given up his vigil and gone out to the byre, thought Peter.

Sam could hardly wait to get into his coat. No breakfast for him! He knew how he would pass the morning – Yule greeting after Yule greeting! – the wind and the boy's shout in every door! In most of the houses Sam would be given a little 'suncake' and a spoon of honey, beside the fire. A penny, perhaps, or a little carved boat, or a pig's bladder for playing football. Miss Alkirk always gave Sam a sixpence, and put her dry mouth to the apple of his cheek.

His mother unbarred the door for him, and kissed him, and let him go.

But when she called Gib for his breakfast of porridge and ale, there was no answer. She went into the boys' room – Gib's bed was empty and cold. In barn and byre, and in the fields round about, there was no sign of him.

Where was Gib? Where was he – the 'trowie one' – where was the bitter cross she had to bear? The folk in the neighbouring crofts hadn't seen him. Peter said, 'That parcel of bread Gib got from Sarah Taing, it isn't in the cupboard. There's three peats missing from the basket. I'm trying to think what he did with the two haddocks I gave him. I think, Mother, Gib's gone to the kirk with his offering.'

But no: Peter and his mother came home from the church white-faced. Gib hadn't been there that day, the beadle assured them.

By noon the whole island knew about the missing boy. Some left their Christmas dinners half-eaten to help in the search. Sam came home weeping. His golden day was in ruins. He loved his strange brother, in spite of everything.

The island was astir with quest and speculation all that afternoon.

While Peter searched one end of the beach, fearful that he might find a grey dear dead face in some pool, the mother at the other end expected any moment to come on a heap of blood and worsted – her own bruised body-fruit – under the crags.

Her anguished steps took her to the cave at last . . .

Inside there was such brightness, such a piercing fragrance, such minglings of pure grave sweet sound, that she cried out and covered her face!

When she took her hands from her eyes at last Gib was sitting on a ledge inside the cave. 'Mam,' he said, 'I wish you had come sooner. They've just gone. They *had* to be off, the man said, before the factor came with his dogs and his gun. The baby was cold.'

Where the light and the incense and the music had been there was nothing – except, on the rocky floor, some hot peat ashes, and a crumb or two, and fishbones.

The sea bride

Cheems lived with his old mother in the tumbledown croft of Mossgar. His father had died when Cheems was a boy. There was a sister, but she had gone in a ship to New Zealand soon after she left school. Sometimes a letter would come from Elinor. Cheems had to read the letter aloud, by lamplight, as best he could; the old woman couldn't read.

Cheems *could* read. That was a very important bit of progress; a divide between the two generations. A school had been built in the centre of the island in the year 1873. A stern schoolmaster from Aberdeen thrashed reading, writing, arithmetic, geography, history, and a little Latin into the young islanders.

Nothing strange was noticed about Cheems of Mossgar in

his schooldays. He was perhaps a little stupid. Nobody, except the schoolmaster, held that against him.

When Cheems was twelve he left school and went to work the croft. He exchanged one kind of drudgery for another. It was about then that a certain queerness was noticed in Cheems.

In those days every crofter was a fisherman also. The few acres about a croft were too small and bare to support a family. Down at the beach the yawls lay. In good fishing weather the work on the land was left to the women. The men rowed west with their creels and lines.

The croft of Mossgar had always shared a fishing boat with the neighbouring croft of Waithe.

One morning Cheems was working in his barn when Howie of Waithe put his head in at the door. 'Drop that flail, Cheems,' he said. 'The bay's alive with mackerel.'

Cheems said he intended to thresh all day.

'Come on!' cried Howie. 'Do you want the other boats to take everything? We're late as it is, man.'

Cheems turned his back on Howie and swung his flail again and again – a dark powerful earth-rhythm.

Howie had to go to the mackerel alone that day.

It turned out that Howie had to go to sea alone every fishing day – whether to the sillocks, the haddocks, the lobsters or the crabs.

'I don't like the sea,' said Cheems in the alehouse. 'I don't like anything about it.'

Because Cheems didn't fish, he and his mother lived rather poorly up at Mossgar. It had never been a well-farmed place at the best of times. Now, as the old woman grew older, the little house and steading came to have a patched withered look about it. A fence, once broken, was never repaired. The gate hung awry from a single rusty hinge. A roofing flag slipped in the stable roof and the rain and the wind came in.

One day the old woman was throwing oatmeal to the hens in the yard. She spoke to them, as she did every day. 'Poor Cheems,' she said. 'The Lord knows what'll come of him. He's a kind of useless cratur. Why can't he go to the fishing? If only you knew, hens, how much I crave for a bit of haddock sweet about the bone, or a crab's claw! His father that's away was as good a fisherman as any. That Howie of Waithe's never paid a penny's compensation for the *Charity*. What'll come of that poor cratur Cheems when I'm in the kirkyard? Why can't he look for a wife?'

It happened that Cheems was working with a fork in the dunghill that day and he heard the monologue. Perhaps he was intended to hear it.

A wife for Mossgar – a young woman about the house – seemed a good idea to Cheems. He sifted over in his mind the half-dozen unattached women in the island. Which one would he ask to be his wife?

That evening after tea Cheems put on his Sabbath suit and set out to visit Bella Swann. He had thought of washing his face, but that seemed too much trouble to take. Bella was a plain hard-working girl. 'Marry you!' she cried when Cheems made his simple proposal in the doorway. 'Lord, it's taken me years to put this house in proper order without starting on your pig-sty of a place!' ... Indeed everything about the house that Cheems cast his eye over shone and glittered: window-panes, doorstep, the brass irons at the fire. 'Besides,' said she, 'I have six men to look after already.'

Cheems left Bella and walked over the hill to the next candidate on his list, Marion Berry. There was a large family of sisters, of whom Marion was the eldest. The girls all clustered in the door as Cheems made his mild proposal to Marion. Marion blushed. One of the sisters gave a titter. Then the whole lobby and threshold was a gale of high-pitched giggles. 'Get away!' cried Marion in a rage.

Where seven innocent faces had been a few seconds before Cheems stared at the quivering oak of the clashed door.

The widow Tarbreck was next on the list. She took Cheems inside, set him down in the fireside chair, brought him a mug of ale. Cheems told her the reason for his coming.

'Now, Cheems,' she said, 'how much money have you got up at Mossgar? Your dad was a careful provident man all the days of him. I warrant there's more than a few sovereigns in that chest under your bed. I wish I could see your family bible – I'm sure there's a pound note folded in most of the pages.'

Cheems said no – there was no treasure like that in the house at all. The only treasure was the few fields and the beasts and himself. The old woman had been a treasure once; now she was old and feeble and cantankerous.

The widow Tarbreck thereupon said she had a washing to do. She bade Cheems a firm good-evening.

Cheems got a rousing reception at the croft of Noust. It was the man of the house, Dod Pow, who came to the door. Cheems made his simple request – could he please have Dod's second daughter Babs for his wife? 'Fetch the shotgun!' roared Dod Pow. 'I swear I've had enough crazy folk at this door. Wife, lock Babs in her bedroom! The gun, quick!'

Cheems had never seen such outrage in a man's face. He moved faster than he had ever moved before. The gun blasted behind him. Pellets scattered about him as he scrambled over the stile between Noust and Banks.

Magda Forss lived alone in a small cottage between the Manse and the Hall. She worked in both those big houses. Nobody knew what the minister's wife or Mistress Alkirk would have done without Magda Forss. Their high mirrors would have been dimmer and their cobwebs would have had time to drift and root and cluster in the rafters.

'Poor Cheems,' she said in answer to his proposal. 'Poor Cheems, go home to your mammy and be a good boy and see you wash your face now and again.'

Cheems was heart-sore with denial. It was getting dark – the sun had been down a half-hour. However, he laid a last mild siege on Merran Smith, forty-five years old, midwife and layer-out of the dead. 'Marry!' came the deep thunder of her voice in the darkening door. 'Marry, is that it? Listen, you, whoever you are. Are you listening? *I hate men.* Have you ever seen the pain and the distress they put on us poor women? Selfish hungry brutes! The only men I like are the corpses I stretch. Don't you imagine for one moment, mister, whoever you are, that I would put up with your non-sense. Wait a minute.' ... Merran went inside and came back with the lamp. 'Mercy!' she cried. 'It's Cheems. If you were the last man on this earth, Cheems, I would say good night to you for ever and ever. GOOD NIGHT.'

For the sixth time that evening Cheems was given a hard door.

He trudged home over the hill, a changed man.

'Have you heard the latest?' said the old woman to the hens one morning soon after that. 'Cheems has got himself a lass. Yes, he has. He won't tell me who she is. She's somebody grand. "She's far too fine and delicate a lady," says Cheems, "to live in the poor croft of Mossgar. So I'm getting a fine house fitted out for her somewhere else. When the house is ready, we're going to live with each other, this lady and me, for ever and ever." ... What lady, I wonder, would look twice at the likes of Cheems? Love's a funny thing. It can't be the laird's daughter – she's in London being educated. I wonder can it be the minister's sister – she's a lady, right enough, but she's sixty if she's a day. Cheems won't say who his sweetheart is. Still, there must be something in it. I never saw such a change in a man. He washes his face in the burn every sunset. He's cut the ragged bits off his beard. He waxed the ends of his moustache last week-end till they're like black needles ... Hens, what am I telling you all this for? You've seen it all yourselves. You know this, he went to Kirkwall one day last week and he came home with a new serge suit and shoes shining like mirrors and a shirt on him white as a shroud ... Love's a fine thing in the beginning, hens. But wait till she starts railing at him! Wait till she gets into debt with the merchants of Kirkwall and the bills start coming in! Some night he'll come home late and staggering from the alehouse – there she'll be standing, with a face on her like thunder, in the doorway ... Love never lasts long.'

The old woman sighed, and threw the last of her oats to the lyrical dipping fluttering hens.

'It won't be long now, hens,' she said. 'Then it'll be only us in Mossgar. Cheems is away all day and every day working on his bride-house.'

Indeed the whole island was amazed at the transformation of Cheems. The man who had recently been 'of the earth, earthy' – bound to the slow uncertain wheel of agriculture, with the earth grained into his face and hands, stooped earthwards under the huge earth-labour – was now suddenly like one of those English dandies who sometimes visited the laird for a week or two in summer. It was true what the old mother had told the hens about the new suit, shirt, and shoes, the coiffure, the daily face-splash in the burn. Cheems, the old woman knew, had been plundering the little hoard of silver that was kept under every croft bed. There was also the new silver watch with the brass chain that one saw whenever Cheems opened his navy-blue serge jacket. There was the new round mirror; that was a secret matter; nobody saw Cheems smirking into it in the privacy of his room, and preening himself like a fine bird on a branch.

Also Cheems, like the toffs from the south, was now utterly idle. He drifted here and there about the island in his holiday clothes at his own sweet will. 'What's doing with thee, boy?' a ploughman would shout as Cheems went past his field. 'Is it not in your field you should be, with ox and plough, this fine day?' ... Cheems would stop and answer mildly that he was finished with farming. He was busy enough, he said, making a house ready for his lass.

Then off the creature would go, while the earth-worker looked after him, and shook his head; and then once more drove the ox summerwards and breadwards.

Cheems's house – everybody in the island spoke and wondered about Cheems's house. There was no sign of any stones being gathered, no sign of a foundation, no sign of rooftree or rafters anywhere in the island.

Howie of Waithe had gone to the shore one day to gather limpets for his fishing next morning when he saw a man standing on a rock, beside a salt water pool at ebb tide, and speaking (it seemed) to vacancy. Howie went closer. The man seemed to be talking through the pool to someone on the far side of the pool, if that were possible. Soon Howie saw that it was Cheems, his neighbour. This surprised him (quite apart from the soliloquy) because Cheems had always had an aversion to the sea and the shore. Howie went as close as he dared, but took care not to be seen. He watched and listened from a coign of the cliff.

Cheems pleaded through the glittering window of the rockpool. 'Come out, lass,' he said. 'It's time, surely. Please.

The house is all but ready. You never saw such a bonny house in all your days. We'll be fine and happy there, just the two of us. Why don't you come out and speak to me? I'm longing to see thee, lass. I know well how busy you are, you and your sisters, sewing the wedding-dress. Still, could you not take five minutes off work and speak to your man? Please. I'm very lonely. I'm sick at the heart, lass, never seeing you at all.' . . .

It was highly comical. No doubt the alehouse would rock with laughter when Howie told that night what he had seen and heard on the beach. But Howie was touched by the sadness of it. Poor Cheems was completely mad now. He imagined himself betrothed to a mermaid! Poor Cheems was hurt because the cold cruel girl would not come out of her sea-palace and kiss him.

'Well, Cheems,' said Howie, 'have you decided to come out fishing in the *Charity* at last? Is this what you're doing, getting limpets from the pool, eh?'

Cheems was very much put out at the sudden inter-ruption. 'Howie,' he said, 'is it you, man? . . . No, I'm not going to the fishing, Howie. I still have some work to do on my house.'

Then he turned his back on Howie and walked away slowly to the opposite side of the bay.

There was loud mirth indeed in the alehouse that night when Howie told his tale. Cheems's love-affair with the mermaid was lingered on beside every croft fire, with wonderment and delight.

But another more sombre mood settled over the island when, a few days later, somebody asked where the great lover was – there had been no sign of him on the roads or fields for a week. The minister went and knocked on the croft door and inquired after Cheems. The old woman said he hadn't been there, for food or sleep, since the previous Thursday. 'He's busy, you see, sir,' she said, 'getting a house ready for the slut, whoever she is, that's taken him away from me.' ...

A week later Howie of Waithe, out with his creels, saw what he took to be a large sack or bolster floating in a drift of seaweed. He urged the *Charity* closer. He turned the heavy bundle over. The drowned face of Cheems looked back at him.

'Christ have mercy,' whispered the fisherman.

The lover had got weary at last of waiting for the beloved. He had secretly opened the door of the sea. He had gone into the bride-chamber to claim the bride.

The day after Cheem's funeral a few daring boys found the house that the simpleton had been preparing for his sea-girl. There was a jam-jar on a ledge of the cave with a few primroses, marigolds, and dandelions drooping out of it. There was a warped table and two chairs. There was a chaff mattress in the deepest secretest part of the cave. There was a sack of peats and a pot and a poker. There was even a framed photograph of Queen Victoria nailed to the wall. There was the crib that Cheems himself had slept and dreamed out his childhood in – and three or four Mossgar generations before him – waiting there for its innocent impossible sea-cold burden.

Oyster fruit

The postman got off his bicycle at the gable-end of the croft of Apgarth. He approached the door with slow solemn strides. He lifted the latch and went in.

Alec Rolfson and his boy Eric were having their breakfast of porridge and milk. They were rather surprised to see the postman. He never called with letters more than two or three times in the year. They weren't overjoyed at sight of the postman either. The postman was a prying fawning self-important creature. 'I am the bearer of the mail – respect me,' his attitude seemed to suggest.

Now he lifted a letter with a heavy red seal on it from the little pile of mail in his fist. ' "Alexander Rolfson, Esq., Apgarth." A very important letter, Alec. Look at the seal. You

must sign for it. I see you have the teapot on the hob.' . . .
The postman sat down on the chair beside the window, erect and vigilant.

'Open the letter, Daddo,' said Eric.

'There's plenty of time,' said his father. 'Leave the letter on the table, Skate. Good-day to you.'

Not only had the postman not been given a cup of tea – he had been insulted. ('Skate' was his nickname.) He left Apgarth, red in the face.

'Bring me my spectacles now, boy,' said Alec.

He poised his steel spectacles on the bulb of his nose. The lenses glinted in the firelight. He ripped open the envelope with the breadknife. He read slowly, carefully, silently.

'What is it, Daddo?' cried Eric. 'Have you been left a fortune? It's time you had some good luck. It must be that cousin in South Africa that's dead, him with the gold-mine.' . . .

'Eric,' said his father, 'you and me, we're as free as the birds. We're as free as birds and fishes. More free, in fact. They have places to nest and shelter in. You and me, boy, it's out in the wind and the rain for us from next Friday on. I wonder, now, could we join a tribe of tinkers?'

'I don't understand,' said Eric. 'What do you mean?'

Thereupon the tenant of Apgarth read the letter to his son. It was from a lawyer in Hamnavoe. Eric couldn't follow all the legal phraseology, but enough to understand that in a few days himself and his father would be homeless. 'Repeated non-payment of rent to Mr Alkirk . . . warning after warning, to no avail . . . a final decision . . . as from the last Friday of May you are to vacate and quit the said premises of Apgarth.' . . .

The couple, man and boy, sipped and swilled till the tea-pot was dry, without saying another word about eviction and homelessness. Alec said, 'I think I'll go and see how the whisky's getting on in the still.' . . . He made whisky once a year in his empty pigsty (though it was against the law). This year's whisky would certainly not be ready before the end of May, or August if it came to that. But Alec spoke, as always, as if he had all eternity before him.

Eric said he thought he might go to the crag for gulls' eggs.

But he did not go towards the crags. Instead he went, in a hushed way, into his room. Beside his bed was a little straw-back chair with a drawer under the seat. In it his mother used to keep her wool and knitting-needles and half-made socks. They were still there, just as the good woman had left them that last winter of her life. Eric rummaged through wool and steel, then he brought out a red spotted handkerchief whose corners were gathered into a knot. He opened it patiently. A little heavy sphere like the moon, like the eye of a blind angel, lay there.

Eric didn't know what it was. One morning last snowtime when the drifts were too heavy for the island children to get to school Eric had wandered down to the shore with Mansie his friend. They had come at last to the famous cave. 'If you go in,' said Mansie to Eric, 'I will too.'

Eric trembled and closed his eyes and went a few steps into the storied darkness. Then he stopped. 'Are you there, Mansie?' he whispered. Mansie was not there. The last of Eric's courage ebbed out of him. Still, he would bring evidence out to Mansie the coward that he had been in the cave and had rummaged among the witch's hoard. He gathered some shell-fish out of the rockpool at his feet. Then he turned and rushed out into the snow-glare and the sea-glitter. 'You coward!' he yelled at Mansie. 'I went right in to the end of the cave, as far as I *could* go. Look!' And he showed his false friend the three oysters.

They often quarrelled, Eric and Mansie. But they were such good friends that after the shouting and five silent seething minutes they would begin to speak to each other again – a few shy surprised words only, as if they were meeting for the first time.

After the latest clash of insults, and a pouting silence, and a wandering back along the beach as if they had nothing to do with each other, really, Eric circled close about his enemy-friend and at last encircled Mansie's neck with his arm. 'We'll sit down on that rock, boy, eh, and open the shells.' ... Mansie said nothing, but sat down on the rock beside Eric – a sign that hostilities, though not entirely at an end, at least were wilting before the dove-branch.

The very first oyster that Eric split with a sharp stone showed the little heavy mysterious moon.

'Isn't it lovely?' cried Eric with delight. He lived in such a rich world! – all these silent treasures of snow that had been emptied over the island while he slept! And now this new strange thing, hidden in an ordinary shell!

'It's nothing,' mumbled Mansie. 'Throw it away.' ... It always took Mansie a good five minutes more than Eric to get over their quarrels.

But Eric put the beautiful thing in his trousers' pocket. Then he and Mansie chased each other along the beach, circling and rushing and shouting, and arrived at last on the shore-road above, breathless and apple-cheeked.

They realized soon that the white air had sharpened their hunger. They smiled to each other. Then they took their separate ways home.

Eric hid his find in the drawer of the straw-back chair.

The general merchant's shop at the crossroads was kept by Ezekiel Tarbreck. There you could buy almost anything from a jar of molasses to a pair of hob-nailed boots. Ezekiel sat at the counter on a tall stool beween his ledge and his till.

Eric's entry was announced by the *ping* of a bell above the door.

Ezekiel looked up from the paper he was reading. 'What have we here?' he said. 'A boy. Why are you not at the school, boy? Oh, Saturday, is that a fact! Come closer, let me see who it is.' . . . He scrutinized the small face across the counter, recognized the boy from the bankrupt croft, and said at once like a trap snapping, 'No tick!'

Slowly Eric undid the red handkerchief and set his 'moon-stone' on the counter.

'What's this?' murmured Ezekiel. 'What have we here?' He picked the thing up and examined it carefully. 'A nothing,' he said at last. 'A disease that shellfish get . . . I hear, boy, that you're very fond of sweeties. Quite right. All boys are fond of sweeties. I was once a boy myself. I'm going to give you a bag of sweeties, boy – peppermints with cloves at the centre of them. They'll keep you sucking and chewing all week-end. Now, how about that? . . . I'll get rid of this sea-thing for you.'

Eric held out his hand.

Ezekiel's long lean fingers trembled as he gave the boy his property. 'It's nothing,' he said. 'I assure you. Valueless. There's a factory in Birmingham that turns them out by the million.'

Eric's next call was to the school-house. Mr MacPhail would know what the thing was. He knew practically every-thing in the world, Mr MacPhail: all the seaports of South America, and all the battles that had ever been fought on the continent of Europe. It was said he could count to a million and beyond.

But Mr MacPhail and his nice wife were not at home. They had gone to Kirkwall for the day, to buy exotic things in the shops there.

It seemed to Eric, lingering on the road outside the school, that it might be best to carry this mystery to the chief man in the island, Mr Alkirk the laird. The boy was troubled and confused. Mr Alkirk, in Eric's experience, was a good kind man. And yet Mr Alkirk, in a week or two, was going to make him and his father homeless. He guessed, on reflection, that Mr Alkirk knew nothing about the situation: it was the factor and the solicitor who had nailed the stern letter of the law to the croft door of Apgarth. It might be that an appeal to the laird from a boy's mouth would salve everything. He reasoned, too, that the mysterious thing he had found might work in his father's favour.

He heard, from Mr West the factor, that Mr Alkirk had left two days before for Edinburgh. Mr Alkirk would be staying in his residence there all summer.

'The Rolfson boy, is it?' said Mr West. 'If that old fox of a father of yours thinks he'll gain anything by sending *you* here, he's making a big mistake. He can thank his lucky stars he wasn't put out on the road the winter before last. He's too lenient, Mr Alkirk – too lenient by half. I hear your father distils too, boy? Let me tell you, if he's caught at that game – making whisky – it's the jail for him. No option.'

All the time Mr West had been pontificating, Eric was struggling with the knot on his grand-dad's snuff handkerchief. At last the little moon glimmered on its scarlet field.

'What's this, boy? You've wasted enough of my time . . . Imm-hmm . . . Ah-ha . . . Where did you get it? In a shell, an oyster? Is that a fact now? In the cave? In a pool in the cave . . . Well, you can go now, boy. I'll look after it. It isn't yours

– you understand that – it was found on the laird's lands – it belongs to Mr Alkirk.' . . .

Eric stood mute, with his open palm held out.

The factor balanced the little sphere in the palm of his own hand, rubbed it between his fingers, held it up to the light, breathed on it, tossed it from one hand to the other.

'Look here, boy,' he said. 'Did your father get a letter this morning – some estate business? He did. Well, he's not to worry about it. It's a legal complication, too difficult for a crofter like him to understand. Go straight home to your father at once and tell him *he's not to worry about it*. His rent is remitted. Of course it is. Mr Alkirk would never countenance an eviction. By no means. The Rolfson family, after all, haven't they been in Apgarth for six or seven generations – two and a half hundred years, I think. Tell your father, as from me, he isn't to worry about his rent for the next five years.'

Eric snatched the treasure from between the enchanted fingers of Mr West. He turned and ran. He had never run faster in his life. He leaped and squelched across the wet peat-land. From time to time he heard the voice behind him. 'Boy, where are you?' . . . 'You're a young fool.' . . . 'You'll find yourself in serious trouble.' . . . 'Come back here at once.' . . .

Eric hid in a black peat-bank until the blundering powerful pursuit went past. 'Boy! . . . Nobody's going to touch you . . . Show yourself.'

When the island was silent again, and the first of twilight lay like pools among the hollows, brimming up silent and brown, Eric went like a shadow homewards. Through the lighted croft window he could see his father eating his supper of fish and bannocks at the scrubbed table.

'Where have you been all day, boy? West was here. I never heard such nonsense out of the man. He seemed to me to be the worse of drink. Something about you, and a treasure out of the sea, and an old honourable peasant family. And Lord knows what else. There's more fish in the pot. The whisky in the sty this year will be good whisky, I think.'

Eric laid the pearl on the table.

His father never uttered a word more. He blew out the lamp. Man and boy, two furtive shadows, they made for the shore and the yawl. In darkness, silent still, they hoisted sail and turned the bow between the islands. Still Alec Rolfson of Apgarth had not said a word when his fist fell on the door of the Kirkwall jeweller.

'Well, Alec,' said Mr Alkirk. 'I hear great and wonderful things have been happening to this island the time I was in Edinburgh.'

'You could say that, sir,' said the tenant of Apgarth.

'A hundred pounds for a pearl,' said the laird. 'What on earth were you thinking of, Alec? In London you'd have got five hundred pounds for a pearl like that.'

'It doesn't matter,' said Alec. 'It was enough to pay my three years' back rent. Now I won't be put out on the road.'

'You wouldn't have been put out on the road in any case,' said Mr Alkirk. 'What kind of a hard-hearted brute do you take me for?'

'I got a very stern letter,' said Alec.

'Listen to me, Alec. You're not a very good crofter, are you? It isn't that you don't work hard. You're unlucky, that's what it is. You sow bad seed – your harvest is always later than other men's harvest, and then as often as not a storm ruins everything.'

'That's a fact,' said the crofter. The two men looked through the window of Apgarth over the district. The Apgarth oats were thin and still green. In other fields the crops stood thick, murmurous in the wind, heavy with the hoarded gold of a long summer. The harvesters were already out in the oatfield of the Glebe. Scythes flashed and fell.

'I'm not going to put you out,' said Mr Alkirk, 'because you happen to be unlucky. You and I are old friends, Alec. I'm not so lucky myself as some of my ancestors. I'm a lot poorer, for one thing. And I hear the government is going to pass some kind of a law about tenants' rights. They're going to cut the rents all round. I'm going to have to pay you compensation for your fences and your bits of draining, and things like that. That means I'll be poorer than ever.'

'Have a dram,' said Alec.

'How much of that hundred pounds have you got left?' said the laird.

'Well,' said Alec, 'not much. I had no sooner paid the back rent than I was summoned to appear at the sheriff court for making illegal whisky. The sheriff fined me fifty pounds.'

'What a shame!' said Mr Alkirk. 'You always made very good whisky, Alec. This stuff is one of your best efforts – pure magic.' ... He sipped, appreciatively, trembling gold circles from a rather filthy cup.

'I managed to hide a dozen bottles,' said Alec. 'That'll see me through the winter. I'll have to think of another hide-out. They know about the pigsty. I'm getting a new copper still made in the smithy. Bressay the blacksmith says it'll be ready before Hallowe'en.'

'Quite right,' said Mr Alkirk. 'I could give you a cellar in the Hall, only West would find out about it for sure. That man is as inquisitive as a bloodhound.'

'I thought of trying the witch's cave.'

'A splendid idea. Nobody would interfere with you there, Alec. Did you say it was in the cave your boy – what's his name – found the pearl?'

'That's where Eric found it.'

'That boy, Eric, he's blessed with the luck you never had, man. I won't live to see it, but when Eric is tenant here at Apgarth there's going to be big yellow harvests in that field of yours.'

'That's the way it goes,' said Alec.

They heard shouts on the hillside. Eric and Mansie were flying a kite. It dawdled and dandled in the big wind over the ripened fields of the island.

The cloud dropper

'I tell you what it is,' said Mrs Jemima Aith, 'they're brutes, every one of them, the Germans. Oh, if I had that Hitler, I would wring his neck for him!'

It was the morning after war was declared. The women of the hamlet on the west side of the island regularly drank tea together in mid-morning, in one house or the other. This morning they broke biscuits and stirred sugar into their tea in the kitchen of Mrs Jemima Aith, a widow with a son.

'If I saw a German floating ashore on a plank of wood,' said Jemima Aith, 'I would – I would . . .' She couldn't think of anything terrible enough to do to the German, but the other women guessed it would be something fierce and final.

'War is a terrible thing!' said Miss Bella Swann the postmistress, and sighed, and took a sip of hot tea.

'They tell me,' said Mrs Wilma Pow whose husband was the island boatman, 'that there are bombs nowadays that can kill a hundred people with one bang.'

'Hitler is quite right,' said Sadie Smith. 'He's done a lot for the German people. We should be fighting on his side against the French.'

They let on not to hear her. They only tolerated the perverse creature because she alone could read the tea-leaves every morning. None of the windfalls, romances, meetings with dark handsome strangers that she predicted ever came to pass; but hope springs eternal; and Sadie Smith probed the future every morning in their empty tea-cups.

'One thing sure,' said Jemima Aith. 'Nolly's going to no war. I'm not having Nolly killed on the battlefields of France like my brother Eric in 1916. Oh no. Nolly bides home with me. They'll take Nolly from me over my dead body.'

Some of the women were of opinion that the sooner Oliver Aith (Nolly) was in the army the better it would be for the whole island. He was an idle useless creature. His old widow of a mother had to keep the thing, even to the extent of cigarettes and week-end beer. It might do him a world of good to be under a sergeant-major for a month or two.

'He'll get called up,' sighed Wilma Pow, 'like my Andy and all the other boys in the island.'

Jemima Aith glared at her. She did not offer Wilma Pow a second cup of tea, though Wilma's cup was empty.

'Germans,' she cried, 'I hate the last one of them! Take another chocolate biscuit, Ada.'

'I will,' said Mrs Ada Bressay. 'It might be the last chocolate biscuit I'll ever eat. There'll be no luxuries from now on. I'm going to stop taking sugar in my tea too. The German submarines will be sinking all the sugar-ships in mid-Atlantic.'

'They will,' said Sadie Smith grimly.

'Nolly dear,' said Jemima Aith to a loutish young man who was leaning with his back to them against the doorpost with a cigarette drooping out of his mouth, 'don't stand there in the draught. You'll catch a cold. That's a good boy. Do what mammy tells you to do. There's still a cup of tea for you, Nolly, in the bottom of the pot.'

Nolly scowled at the women over his shoulder. He didn't move. Ashes spilled from his cigarette over the scrubbed doorstep . . .

Sadie Smith saw in Bella Swann's cup a red-haired good-looking stranger. Bella blushed, and smiled, and shook her head. Sadie saw in Wilma Pow's cup a sack of money – quite a lot, in fact – it looked as if she might come up in the football pools. 'I don't do them,' said Wilma Pow firmly.

Little Seenie Berry had swallowed all her tea-leaves. 'You're a fool,' said the fortune-teller. 'You're always swallowing your tea-leaves.' . . . 'Nothing ever happens to me, anyway,' said little Seenie.

In Mrs Ada Bressay's cup was a crib, and not only a crib but a pram, and not only a crib and a pram but an infant's rattle, bottle and pottie. This was curious, because Ada Bressay the kirk organist had been married for ten years to Ron Bressay the blacksmith, without issue. It appeared unlikely that the marriage was to be blessed now with a baby. Ada glanced into her cup that Sadie Smith was holding up for all to see. 'I don't see any of them things,' she said.

'You don't,' said Sadie Smith. 'You haven't got the gift.' And she pushed the black lace of tea-leaves inside the bowl with a blunt forefinger. 'Time up,' she said. 'I've got my work to do. Somebody'll have to be ready to welcome the Jerries when they come.'

'The tramps,' said Jemima Aith. 'They won't come here. Orkney is too far for them. You forgot to read my cup.'

Sadie glanced swiftly into the clay hollow in Jemima's hand.

'There's nothing much,' she said. 'An aeroplane.'

'I'll maybe be taking a "flip" to see my brother Sandy in Kirkwall,' said Jemima. 'Myself and poor Nolly. A change would do him good.' (There was an inter-island air service.)

'No,' said Sadie Smith, 'but it's a very big plane, and there are things falling out of it.'

Winter darkened and stormed upon the islands, and the war went on (though some of the women in the hamlet thought it would be over by Christmas).

An exciting thing happened in mid-November. Soldiers arrived in the island, mostly English. They lived in tents to begin with, but the Irish labourers who arrived soon after built a cluster of wooden huts to shelter them. At the same time a great searchlight emplacement of reinforced concrete was built near the edge of the cliffs to the west.

Soon the islanders (especially the women) and the soldiers were on the best of terms with each other.

'Searchlights,' said Jemima Aith. 'What a waste of time and money! What are they expecting to find with their lights?' This she said on the first night the searchlight was switched on. A long powerful beam probed the depths of the sky, and moved here and there. It was answered silently by searchlights from other islands. Sometimes the slim pencils of light would come together in one luminous deadly point, sometimes they formed a mesh through which nothing alien could conceivably pass unobserved.

The soldiers had a pleasant mess-hut where they drank beer in the evenings, and played darts and housie-housie. The islanders were cordially invited to be present. There it was observed that Bella Swann was often in the company of a good-looking corporal from Gloucester, called Sammy Gresham. Sammy had vivid red hair.

It was observed too that Nolly Aith spent evening after evening leaning against the bar. But nobody was really surprised at that. 'Nolly's delicate,' said his mother. 'A drop of beer won't hurt him.'

Otherwise the only way the war affected the island was that many delectable things were rationed, such as sugar and bread and jam. There was also meat rationing, bacon rationing, and egg rationing; but that hardly touched the stomachs of an island teeming with agricultural produce. There was so much to spare that the island farms did a brisk regular trade with the soldiers from the searchlight. Thousands of eggs and chickens and round white cheeses were despatched to households in London, Liverpool, Birmingham. Bella Swann up in the post office had never handled so many parcels.

The best provider of farm produce to the soldiers was Wilma Pow. Her man Tom was the island boatman. He was rather lazy and so didn't bring in much money. But Wilma Pow had inherited a little croft from her uncle. Between croft and ferry-boat the couple normally managed to scrape along and provide for a growing family. Now Wilma, in these dangerous times, husbanded her resources and worked twice as hard. She drove the tractor herself, to peat-hill and ploughing. The number of her hens increased twenty-fold; always there was a red and white flurry about her door as the soldiers came with their empty egg-boxes for replenishment. Wilma bargained with the mess sergeant about the kitchen left-overs up at the camp; she began to keep pigs on the bucketfuls of swill she got every day ... In short, Wilma Pow soon had more money in the box under her bed than she had ever seen in her life before.

Bella Swann took to walking with her red-headed hero along the lonely island roads. 'Aha,' said the wise ones, 'there's an understanding there!' ... Some of the younger ones who read magazines spoke of 'a romance'. The island post office was suddenly a pleasant place to do business in.

Seenie Berry, the girl who swallowed tea-leaves with tea, was quite unmoved by the soldiers. Or rather, she had nothing to do with those strangers in her close proximity. But all through the winter she sat at home knitting khaki balaclavas and khaki gloves for soldiers in France that she had never seen.

Jemima Aith watched with some unease the growing restlessness in Nolly. A discontent had fallen on him. Sometimes, after wheedling an extra half-crown out of her, he would come home drunk from the army camp. Sometimes he would sit in moody silence beside the fire, days on end.

All winter Sadie Smith the seamstress predicted that the Germans were playing with the British and the French. Soon they would strike, and then the allies would be like a sheet of glass under a forge hammer.

'Bad cess to them!' cried Jemima Aith. 'I wish I had my hands on that fat Goering! I'd melt him down for candles.'

The long dark winter passed. Then, one morning in February, the island saw a doleful sight – Mrs Jemima Aith lamenting from door to door of the hamlet. They finally got to the source of her woe – the darling one, the joy of her heart, the good-for-nothing layabout Nolly had disappeared. 'There's been this darkness on his mind,' she wailed. 'It's gotten worse lately. The Germans, I blame them. Oh, if I got my hands on them! My boy'll be found at the foot of the cliffs, broken.'

The mystery was explained a few days later. A postcard with a few crude words on it arrived at the Aith house. Nolly

117

had slipped off to Kirkwall and joined a merchant ship. He was bored in the island, he wrote to his mother. He wanted to see a bit of excitement. Mrs Jemima Aith smiled through her tears. 'I'm proud of my Nolly,' she said. 'What a brave boy! The Germans had better watch out now.'

The women were all sitting one day, as usual, drinking their morning tea. This day the session was up at the post office. The mail had been dispatched in Tommy Pow's boat – Bella Swann had an hour to draw her breath, put the kettle on the stove, arrange chairs for her visitors and cups and cakes, and even to comfort Jemima Aith somewhat.

'What's that on your finger?' said Wilma Pow to Bella Swann.

Bella blushed. It was a gold engagement ring with a diamond in it.

They all hastened to congratulate her, some with more enthusiasm than others. 'You're lucky,' said Ada Bressay. 'He's a fine lad, that Sammy Gresham.'

'You'll be the next to be hooked,' said Wilma Pow to Seenie Berry.

'No, I won't,' said Seenie Berry. 'I don't speak to soldiers. I only knit for the ones in the Maginot Line.'

Sadie Smith muttered darkly that soon there would be no Maginot Line. Seenie should be saving her wool for the hard defeated times that were coming.

It was then that Jemima Aith turned on her neighbour; fired perhaps by the fact that her Nolly was now on active service. 'You watch yourself!' she cried. 'Keep a lock and key on your tongue. Don't think you aren't being watched – yes, and listened to – and spoken about by them in authority, the security folk. Maybe you've never heard of Regulation 18B. Well, madam, a few more words out of you, like what you've been saying all winter, and you'll find yourself behind fortress bars! You will.'

There was no reading of the tea-leaves that morning. Highly offended, Sadie Smith put down her half-eaten biscuit and was out of the door like a hare out of a hutch.

'Well done, Jemima,' said Wilma Pow. 'I've often wanted to say just that to the creature but I've never had the courage.'

'That might be the last cup-reading in this island till the war's over,' said Bella Swann, turning the ring on her finger till the diamond caught the light. 'A pity in a way.'

'I won't miss it,' said Seenie Berry. 'Nothing ever happens to me, thank goodness, anyway.'

'She's a very good cup-reader, too,' said Mrs Ada Bressay. 'You remember that morning just after the war started. She saw a red-headed man in Bella's cup. And she saw a bag of money in Wilma's cup.'

'What I earn by my own efforts is no concern of anybody,' said Wilma Pow rather tartly.

'And she saw an aeroplane in Jemima's cup,' went on Ada Bressay.

'Well, that was wrong,' said Jemima. 'Nolly – the Lord look after him well, the innocent thing that he is – is in the merchant navy, not in the Air Force.'

'And she saw – in my cup – she saw – she . . .' Ada was confused. She hung her head. She blushed. Even the backs of her hands grew red.

'I remember,' shrilled Seenie. 'She saw a pram and a crib!'

Four astounded pleased faces looked round at the glowing woman in their midst.

'Ada,' cried Wilma Pow. 'You can't mean – after all this time, Ada – can it be true!'

'Yes,' murmured Ada Bressay. 'The smithy is going to be blessed, round about midsummer, with a baby.'

From time to time, ever since the beginning of the war, the

islanders would hear a high remote insect-drone in the sky. Presently it would falter and fade away. It was of course an aeroplane, and it sounded different from the British planes that swarmed everywhere about the sky. 'A German bomber,' the islanders remarked to each other, and nodded. The soldiers said nothing; they had been told to keep their mouths closed. 'Careless Talk Costs Lives' – that slogan was everywhere, on posters in the village hall, the church porch, the door of the grocery van.

Whenever the faint wavering drone was heard after sunset, every searchlight in Orkney spanned the sky, silently, shifting, parting, converging – like a blind bright cat after the smell of a mouse. The islanders were proud of the great probing beam that was rooted in their own island. It was so bright it made the stars like specks of ash – it made the moon a cinder. There was a nation-wide blackout, of course. It was as if all the forbidden lights of the island – the tilley lamps and the paraffin lamps and the wind-generated electric lamps – had gone to feed that searchlight on the edge of the cliffs.

'Oh,' cried Jemima Aith. 'I hate them! Invading *our* sky, if you please! The limmers – nothing's too bad for the likes of them!'

In the hamlet the supper tables had just been cleared, when the faint pulsing drone was heard again. It was an evening in March. 'They're early tonight,' said Wilma Pow to Tom Pow. The Pow children rushed to the door. The Pow hens wandered about the yard, pecking at stone, and root, quite indifferent to that vague sky-murmur. A violent voice echoed from the battery a hundred yards above. 'Go indoors, there! Do you want to be killed?'

It was the sergeant-major. He was a stern man by nature, but the islanders had never heard such a lion-roar out of him.

Old Mrs Berry, Seenie's mother, said in her doorway, 'The impudence, telling *us* what to do in our own island – him, a ferry-lowper!'

The islanders mutely defied Sergeant-Major Kane, lingering in open doors and at gable-ends, their faces sky-tilted and pink in the westering sun. There was nothing to be seen. The German bomber must be flying very high.

'The German bombers' I should have said, for it was no single drone this time, there was a denser pulsing, a weave of ominous sound deep in the south-east segment of sky.

Certain of the Orkney islands enclose a grey stretch of water that became in war-time a famous naval base; there the great ships of the British Navy came and bunkered and left again. It was of course that harbour, called Scapa Flow, that the Luftwaffe was interested in. All through the winter those solitary spy-planes had come to see what great ships were lying at anchor ... The fabric of noise above shredded thin.

'They're turning back,' cried Jemima Aith. 'The cowards! The scum!'

Sergeant-Major Kane's face was as red, in the sunset, as a turnip lantern.

'I tell you why the sergeant-major's wild,' said Tom Pow to Wilma Pow. 'He can't show off his searchlight. The Jerries are away home for their supper in the last of the light.'

That was the last word that was heard in the island for an hour or more. Suddenly the whole world erupted with fire and smoke and thunder. The anti-aircraft guns on Selskay and Norday flamed and stabbed. All round the broad shores of the naval base – hidden from this island – the guns hurled their shells skyward at the raiders. The sun was down. In the growing twilight the mouths of the guns spat crimson ruin. Little clusters of puffballs appeared here and there in the sky to the south-east. 'Oh Lord,' cried old Mrs Berry, 'the Germans are coming down in their parasols! Hide under the bed, Seenie. This is the end of us.'

But Seenie told her mother not to be silly. It wasn't parachutes at all, but the anti-aircraft shells exploding. 'Don't be frightened, Mam. Nothing ever happens to us.'

The whole island was shuddering now from the din. In brief intervals of silence they heard the menacing throb of the bombers. Then once more the anti-aircraft guns cried against them with scarlet mouths.

There was a series of distant thuds. Bombs were falling among the aircraft carriers and the cruisers in Scapa Flow.

Now, with darkness, a new silent spectacular chorus entered the cosmic drama – the searchlights. They swept about the darkening sky-dome; they meshed, scissored, came together in a dazzling cone right over Selskay. And there, in that intolerable focus of light, an aeroplane hung. It traversed the sky slowly. It was sighted, but not yet trapped. The guns, an earth-rooted pack, yelped around it. The bomber was making for home, if it could only escape out of this cage of light and fire. Inexorably the score of searchlights tracked it down the sky.

Then the islanders saw the enemy plane tilt, stagger, flower into flame, falter. The searchlights lost it, so fast it fell out of the sky on to the only hill in the island. The island shook from the impact. The hill blazed with its pyre. There in the sky, like two serene dancers, parachutes drifted down.

The bomber, when the soldiers and crofters reached it, was a charred ruin. The bodies of two men were taken from the hot metal and the smoke. Clement Maclean of Waithe croft arrested one of the parachutists with his pitchfork and marched him along to the searchlight battery, where he was received grimly by Sergeant-Major Kane.

The spring night was quiet and dark again, and sweet with the smell of dew and young sleeping flowers.

'There were *two* parachutes,' said Tom Pow. Soldiers and islanders spent the whole night combing the island from end to end. They found the second parachute in the oatfield of Garth, discarded. 'My,' cried Bella Swann, 'what a beautiful wedding nightgown I could make out of it!' Mrs Ada Bressay wanted it for a christening robe for her first baby. In the end the fine fabric was divided between them. There was plenty of material for both.

The men of the island searched and probed every nook and corner, from the erne eyrie to the lowest ebb-tide pool. It was difficult in the darkness without lanterns. The enemy airman eluded the net time after time. In daylight, of course, his capture was certain.

The women spent a night of delicious terror. What if the door were to open – and they alone in the house with their bairns – and a blond brute with a tommy-gun were to come strutting in! 'Lord preserve us and keep us,' prayed old Mrs Berry. 'Seenie, lie close beside me. Did you bar the door?' ... 'It's all right, Mam,' said Seenie. 'Nothing ever happens to us.' She added under her breath, 'More's the pity!' and sighed.

Sadie Smith stood the whole night behind her door with an axe in both her shaking hands.

At dawn, Ada Bressay's man, Ron the blacksmith, turned to Second-Lieutenant Wilcox and said, 'We've been fools. He's in the cave, of course. That's where we should have looked in the first place.'

In the cave they found their man. He was drinking tea with Mrs Jemima Aith, and eating the rock-cakes that she baked better than any other woman in the island. They were sitting together on a ledge. Jemima Aith was telling the fair-haired blue-eyed boy all about her Nolly – the things that Nolly had said and done from his infancy; and how the island was too small a place for the likes of Nolly; and Nolly, now that he had chosen the sea for a career, would most likely end up as a ship's officer or even a commodore.

The airman had one leg stretched along the cave ledge – he was obviously in pain.

Jemima Aith was just pouring another cup of tea, from her thermos, for the German navigator, her guest, when the search party entered the cave.

The prisoner surrendered, smiling. 'This lady,' he said, 'has been good to me, like my own mother. She has sat with me all night. She brews delicious tea. She has bandaged my ankle. I caught my foot in a furrow, coming down.'

They let him finish his tea before they led him, hirpling, away.

The end of the cave

'Oh dear,' said Mrs Taing in the kitchen of the Hall, 'he's in a bad mood this morning again. Just listen.'

Solveig, Mrs Taing's daughter, aged twelve, stopped her work with cake and candles for a second or two. 'The poor skipper,' she said. 'It's his gout.'

There was a mumbling and a grumbling from upstairs.

'If he drank less gin,' said Mrs Taing tartly, 'he would have less gout. No – it's since "The Orcadian" came last Saturday that he's been carrying on.'

It seemed, from the local paper, that ten years previously geologists had discovered some valuable unspecified mineral – silver or uranium – in the north-west corner of the island;

no scant traces either, but thick rich seams of the stuff. Now there was an urgent plan afoot – in the interests it was said of the national prosperity, or even survival – to exploit this treasure. In the Islands Council permission had been given to a mining company to begin preliminary probing and blasting.

Some councillors, said the newspaper report, had had reservations. A beautiful unspoiled coast-line would be ruined – in particular a certain cave into which much island lore and history were gathered. But the councillor from the island itself, Mr William Tarbreck, had made mincemeat of the objection – 'A filthy smelly frightening place!' he had declared to the Council. ' "The Witch's Cave" – that's what we call it in the island. Some hideous old hag called Jenny, a long long time ago, she cooked children and drank their blood in the cave (or so the story goes). In my opinion, the island would be well rid of that black hole. Are we to let an eyesore like that stand in the way of Progress, gentlemen? The island I have the honour to represent is now rich beyond what any of us dreamed. Let us take the gifts that Providence has hidden away for our benefit, from the beginning, in the barren places of the island!'

That speech, said the newspaper, had been greeted with loud and prolonged applause . . .

There came a blast – the sound of an explosion – from the rugged north-west shore of the island. The rifling had begun.

The distant blast was echoed by the shouts of an old man from upstairs. 'This is it! The ruination of the island! That Willie Bubblenose – if I could put my stick on his back!'

'Isn't it a shame,' whispered Solveig, 'and this his birthday?'

'The bad-tempered thing that he is,' said Mrs Taing. 'Twice last week I nearly gave in my notice. I won't put up with it much longer.'

Solveig said nothing. She knew her mother would never do such a thing. She had too high a regard for Captain Sigurd Bressay, bad temper, gout, swear-words and all. As for Solveig herself, she would be broken-hearted if they ever left the Hall – that beautiful old house – to go back to the tumbledown croft of Smelt. Besides, how would the skipper ever manage without them?

Solveig went on sticking tiny blue and red and yellow candles in Captain Bressay's birthday cake which Mrs Taing had baked in secret the previous week. It was a beautiful cake, shaped like a ship, with funnel, bridge and port-holes – a white immaculate ship to make the mouth of an old master-mariner water, and his heart rejoice.

'Solveig,' said Mrs Taing,' 'I can hardly see the cake now for candles.'

But Solveig was determined to root sixty-three candles in the cake. Captain Bressay loved colours and candle-flames.

There was another blast from two miles away.

'The scum!' came the roar from upstairs.

'A letter came for him an hour ago,' sighed Mrs Taing over the potato peelings. 'Looks like a birthday card. A Kirkwall postmark. Take it up to him. That might cheer him up.'

Solveig put a last scarlet candle in the stern of the ship-cake and went upstairs with the letter to Captain Bressay's room.

Sigurd Bressay – haven't we heard the name 'Sigurd' in this book already, right at the beginning? And, at the time of the German air-raid, wasn't there a Mrs Ada Bressay who was expecting a baby, greatly to her joy, after ten fruitless years of marriage? This choleric old man who lived up at the Hall was the same sweet secret expectation, the same lonely boy who had wandered about the shores of the island half-a-century before and spoken to the seals.

It is time now for some details of Sigurd Bressay's life to be filled in.

Seven weeks after he was given the treasury of cave stories by Shelmark, Sigurd left the island school, along with three or four of his brighter contemporaries, and went to the senior school in Hamnavoe. He was a clever enough boy, especially at English and history and geography. At last, when he was about sixteen, he had to make up his mind what career to follow. And that was a problem, because the boy never seemed to know his mind for two days on end. His shoulder was too white and delicate to wield an anvil-hammer. Fate, or Chance, or his Good Angel decided the matter. A Grimsby trawler sheltered one January day in the harbour of Hamnavoe from a black westerly gale. It was a Saturday afternoon. Sigurd and two other boys wandered down the long pier to have a look at the smart powerful new ship that could sail round Iceland and even as far as the North Cape – so very different from the rusty battered trawlers that had used to shelter in Hamnavoe in the old days. The boys were invited on board by the mate, and shown round the ship. Sigurd's friends spent a fascinated hour down in the engine-room, but Sigurd was more interested in the bosun, an old leather-skinned crinkly-eyed man, heraldic with tattoos up to his shoulders. This man and Sigurd sat on a coil of rope, and Sigurd listened open-mouthed to the terrible and heroic sagas of the North Atlantic convoys during the war. (Sigurd loved stories more than anything else in the world.) The bosun offered Sigurd a chew of tobacco – Sigurd shook his head. He told Sigurd how he had been thrice torpedoed, the second time in the Arctic Ocean, carrying tanks to Russia; the water had been so cold that he could feel his heart turning to ice inside him. Then the German bombers roared out of the south, and machine-gun bullets fretted the sea like spatters of hot hail among the drowning ice-men . . .

At this point Sigurd was aware of a throb through the trawler, a regular pulsation, a heart-beat; and the soft hissing of cloven waters. When he looked through the port-hole, there were the great red cliffs of Hoy on the portside, and to starboard the open Atlantic.

'Well,' said the bosun, 'right enough I was more a block of ice than a seaman when they picked me up. I thought, when I saw the rum-bottle, I was going to get some central heating, and I'm telling you this, boy, my heart thawed a little at the prospect. No such luck, they started to rub me all over with the good stuff – a pure waste. Still, I suppose it was the saving of me.'

'My Aunt Maggie,' said Sigurd,' 'will be pouring out my soup. She'll be wondering why I'm late for my dinner.'

The trawler skipper refused to return to Hamnavoe with the boy. He said they had wasted enough time. The storm was over, there were fish to be caught. In the three days following, off Rockall, they drew an immense silver treasure out of the sea, and then, freighted with cod, turned and made for Fleetwood. Sigurd was not allowed to idle; the stowaway's job was to polish everything shiny about the ship. In the evenings he sat on that coil of rope and listened to the bosun's stories. ('What a liar that bosun is,' said the cook to Sigurd in the galley. 'He's told his lies so often he's come to believe them.') Lies or truth, Sigurd's ears brimmed with the magic of them: Bombay, Saigon, Singapore, New York, Melbourne. Once, absent-mindedly – because this particular story was so good, Chinese pirates off Formosa – Sigurd accepted a sliver of bogey roll and put it between his teeth. He grew rigid and green with the poisonous juice that trickled down his throat. But even that experience didn't disenchant him with the bosun; who, it transpired as this latest tale unfolded, was captured by the yellow pirates, and tortured dreadfully with small cunning razor-sharp cuts in various parts of his body as he lay spread-eagled and staked down in the courtyard of the Chinese pirate-chief. 'Another ten cuts,' said the bosun, 'and I'd have been a gonner, boy. The torturers were beginning to slice all around my heart. Didn't the pirate-chief's daughter come on the scene just at that point, and take pity on me, and beg her father to spare me! They sealed up the cuts with honey and resin, and me being a healthy young son-of-a-gun I soon recovered. In the month of the lotus – that's what they call July in them parts, boy – me and this Chinese girl got spliced. Of course I didn't tell her I was married four times already.'

Sigurd Bressay was put ashore in Fleetwood, and given money for his passage back to Orkney.

What though he got a wallop on the side of his head from Aunty Maggie when he stepped through her door at Hamnavoe, and immediately afterwards, from the same source, several kisses and tears all over his face? What though he was taken to the police-station and interrogated sternly by the sergeant as to all the circumstances of his adventure? What though the old women at the close-ends shook their heads whenever Sigurd went past, and said that boy would come to a poor end? One thing was clear and settled in Sigurd's mind. He would go to sea when he left school. Those three stowaway days and nights had put the enchantment of salt and horizons on him.

For a month or two he was a hero among his schoolmates. But that was a role that he had no relish for. He remained a solitary boy, as always; he spent most of his evenings reading Conrad, Hakluyt, and *The Log of the Blue Dragon*.

There is not enough space to chart Sigurd Bressay's career at sea. That would take a half-dozen books to tell. He was moderately successful. While still a young man he gained his master mariner's ticket. He must have put twenty circles round the watery globe before his temples began to grey. Whenever he got leave he came back to the island; now his parents were growing old; and at last his father was not able to work at the forge and anvil. In mid-Pacific one voyage a radio message came to him – his father, that powerful dark sweet-natured man, had died. There was nothing that could be done about it, at such a remove. As soon as his ship reached Liverpool, Sigurd took an urgent train north. It was two graves, not one, that he stood in front of with bowed head; for he learned that his mother had outlived his father by only three weeks, so close their existences had been thirled to each other.

Sigurd left the house and smithy to decay. Nobody needed them. The island was slowly being drained of its people, like all the lonely places of the earth. And as for forge and anvil, the great plough-horses were all gathered now into legend. The tractor was lord of the fields.

Sigurd reckoned he had a quarter of a century of sea-life yet before he could retire. He promised himself that then, with his accumulated savings (he had no wife or children) he would return to the island, and restore his parents' croft, and so live out in peace the rest of his days.

But prophets and poets have said profound things about mice and men, and all their careful vain thought for the morrow. Captain Bressay had never been a very robust man. Like some solitaries he was inclined to tilt the bottle more often than was good for him; many a day the ship's crew heard the morning-after growl and grate in his throat. Sometimes there were such flashings of pain in his left foot that he could only hobble about on his bridge with difficulty and a sweat-silvered face. Whenever his gout got too bad he was given generous leave of absence; he being a valued servant of the shipping line.

Mrs Taing, advised by letter of his imminent arrival, would strive for days to get the old smithy-house aired and heated and provisioned for him. He refused to stay in any other house. 'He's too mean, old Bressay,' the islanders said. And indeed, like many ageing bachelors, Sigurd Bressay consulted his various bank books and building society books with the reverence sometimes accorded to holy writ. In an idle moment, to pass the time, he would dredge out of his pocket all his loose change, silver and copper, and count them the way an anchorite might tell his beads.

After a few summers of increasing rot and draughts and dampness, Mrs Taing said flatly to Captain Sigurd Bressay that the smithy-house was hardly better than a pigsty. He would catch his death if he were to spend another leave of bad weather in it – 'and you not strong, and with that swollen foot, and getting no younger.'

It happened that same year that the last of the ancient family of the Alkirks died, who had been lairds in the island nearly five hundred years. She was a gentle old spinster called Miss Mavis Alkirk, and she spent what was left of a considerable fortune on the island and its people – building from her own funds a community centre, putting a new roof on the kirk (and an organ and a steeple and a mellow-tongued bell at the same time, though she was an Episcopalian). If an old man fell sick and refused to go to the Old Folks' Home in Kirkwall or Hamnavoe, she would nurse him till he was better, even to the extent of doing the most unpleasant things for his comfort. If a fisherman drowned, there would be an anonymous gift to widow and orphans far in excess of the community subscription. She died, the old lady, among her flowers, one summer evening late, when the scents and perfumes are at their heaviest and richest.

Occasionally, like some penny-pinching folk, Captain Bressay indulged in a wild splurge, as if he was Captain

Henry Morgan and had a hidden hoard of doubloons and escudos somewhere in Jamaica or Haiti. Mrs Taing (with Solveig a small thing clinging to her skirts) told him one morning about the death of Miss Mavis Alkirk, 'an angel and a saint if ever there was one'. Captain Bressay, seated on a broken chair in the old smithy-house, got a sudden gleam in his eye – he said at once that he would buy the Hall. It didn't matter how much it cost, he had enough put by for it, he told Mrs Taing. That same afternoon he telephoned the Alkirk solicitors in Edinburgh. Within a week all was settled – the huge house in the centre of the island was his.

'Lookee here, woman,' he said to Mrs Taing, 'the sea's getting too much for me. The next voyage will be the last voyage. This foot of mine's getting worse. If I was a blind man, some days I would swear my hoof was a raging fire from toes to ankle. Don't want to end my days on a crutch. I'll have a fine quiet life of it up there at the Hall.'

'Hall or hovel,' said Mrs Taing, 'if you don't stop that gin-drinking there'll be flames and burnings in more than your foot. I would hate to see that liver of yours.'

'Mind your own blasted business!' said the captain. 'I want you to have that Hall in decent order for me when I come home for good. That'll be in October. What's the name of that child?'

'Solveig,' said Mrs Taing.

'A credit to you, a credit to you ... Mrs Taing, you'll oblige me, seeing that I have only half a bottle left, by getting a case of gin from Willie Tarbreck the licensed grocer. Put it down to my account. Outrageous, what that man charges for his drink.'

So, at the age of sixty-two, Captain Sigurd Bressay, a hirpling brick-faced fleck-bearded impatient man, came to settle down for ever in the quiet island out of whose dust he had been formed, into whose dust he would be mingled at last.

Nobody greatly cared for him in the island except Solveig Taing, the plain-faced girl who helped her mother by cleaning the cutlery in the Hall kitchen, and peeling potatoes and such-like tasks. Often on a cold winter afternoon she would have to mix Captain Bressay's toddies for him, and sometimes read *The Scotsman* or *The Guardian* to him as he swayed back and fore in his rocking-chair, snorting and swearing at some particularly outrageous piece of news – such as, that the Americans had launched another space probe ('Silly damn fools – useless expense!') or that the Glasgow dustmen on strike were letting thousands of tons of rat-infested garbage rot on the streets of that tumultuous city. ('Should be damn glad they have a job to go to! Communists at the root of it – Reds!')

The islanders wondered at Mrs Taing, that hard-working woman, putting up with the bad-tempered old creature. 'And,' said old woman to old woman at the grocery van, 'he only pays her five pounds a week. A skinflint. That Andrina Taing just slaves out her life for him. If I was Andrina Taing I would go home to Smelt tomorrow. I would.' . . . But what they could understand least of all was how Mrs Taing allowed an innocent bairn like Solveig to have her ears abused by utterances that might make a tinker blush. The odd thing was, the girl was neither shocked nor hurt. Indeed, Solveig was the only living person the old mariner had any regard for. If ever his face seemed like a turnip-lantern with rage or gin, or his foot shimmered with the intense invisible fires of gout, it was that girl with the freckles on her nose and the mouse-coloured hair that alone could infuse a pinch of sweetness into him.

What bound the old man and the girl together was the cave and its treasury of stories. He would tell her, over and over again, the stories of the cave, as she sat on the carpet beside his rocking-chair.

'What a clever man you are, skipper,' she said once, 'to think up such stories.'

'Me think them up!' he shouted. 'A louse has more imagination than me. I'm telling you the stories as I heard them from Shelmark the seal.'

'Is it true, skipper, that you played games with the seals in the sea?'

'Yes, all the last summer I was a boy.'

'Did you ever kiss a seal-girl behind a rock?'

'Time for my toddy, Solveig. You put too much water and not enough honey in the last cup.'

Captain Bressay opened the letter Solveig brought up and said, 'Holy blazes, it's my birthday! I forgot. How old does that make me, Solveig?'

'Sixty-three,' said Solveig.

'What a clever girl you are,' said the captain. 'This morning, when I heard the blasting, I felt like ninety-nine. That Willie Tarbreck our councillor – he's the same age as me, Solveig, we were at school together, him and his "progress" and his "witch's cave" where babies were stewed and had their hearts tapped – he always had bubbles at his nose, that Willie, and he wiped them on the sleeve of his jersey – a dreadful boy altogether – whenever I think of Willie I feel like a hundred and six. But you, Solveig, when you're in the room I feel – let me see – about fifteen again.'

'Who's the birthday card from, skipper?'

'My second cousin Claudia. The only relation I have left in the world. Lives in Kirkwall. Would you believe it – she's coming to see me this afternoon – crossing over on Voe's ferry-boat, if you please, with a present for me.'

135

'Nice, skipper.'

'Nice my flaming foot! Did you ever have words with that same Claudia, my cousin?'

'I've never seen her, skipper.'

'Don't like the woman. I know why she's coming. She thinks I have thousands stashed away in the bank, besides this big house. If I pop off, as I could easily do if the fire in my foot and the fire in my liver were to build up a big head of steam – well then, thinks Claudia, "All Sigurd's immense wealth will be coming to me, so I might as well be nice to him in the short time that's left ..." I'm telling you this, girl, I would like to see Claudia's face when the will's read out.'

There was a sequence of three explosions, one after the other, from the cliff.

'The yellow-bellies!' the old man roared. 'They're killing the island! This is the end.'

'Solveig,' came her mother's voice from downstairs, 'I need you in the kitchen at once.'

'A happy happy birthday, anyway, skipper,' said Solveig, and kissed him on his furnace of a cheek.

'Thank you, dear. Tell your mother I want nothing special for my supper, no cakes and nonsense like that. Can't afford it. And, Solveig?'

'Yes, skipper.'

'When Claudia comes, to observe with joy the shadows gathering about me, you're to tell her that I'm feeling very low today and would she please not bide for more than ten minutes.'

'All right, skipper.'

'Solveig, before the sun goes down would you walk as far as the cliff and see what that dynamite's done to our sky-line?'

'I will.'

'Seeing that it's my birthday, Solveig, will you do something special for me?'

'Anything, skipper.'

'You'll find a new bottle of gin in the cupboard there. Pour half a cupful.'

'My mam says I'm to do no such thing.'

'Your mam knows nothing. Don't know how I put up with her. A man who's been staked down by yellow Chinese pirates and had nine hundred and ninety cuts in him, he needs an occasional cup of gin. A man who's been sunk in the Arctic and felt his heart turning to ice inside him, who would grudge that man a little refreshment? Your mother's a stupid woman. Don't put too much water in. Tilt the bottle some more.'

While Solveig was pouring the gin into the cup, there was a fifth reverberation from the north-east corner of the island. 'Blast them!' roared Captain Bressay. 'The black pit rot them!'

Miss Claudia Bressay knocked at the Hall door at half past two. She had a parcel in her hand, coloured paper, neatly taped and tied. 'How is Sigurd?' she said in the door to Mrs Taing, her voice as sweet as a lemon.

'The same as usual. Swearing, drinking, grumbling,' said the housekeeper.

'It must be two years since I saw him,' said Claudia. 'You know, Mrs Taing, Sigurd and I are the only Bressays left in Orkney. We were always close to each other. Did he get my card? I was determined to come and see him today. How is his poor gout? I have a little something here for him that'll be soft and comfortable on his feet.'

'You'd better come upstairs then,' said Mrs Taing.

'Not more than ten minutes,' said Solveig. 'The captain said to tell you that.'

'Ten minutes!' said Miss Bressay. 'I have hundreds of things to say to Sigurd. Where is the silver plate that used to hang on that panel there – a very valuable piece?'

'He sold it to Tarbreck for a crate of burgundy,' said Mrs Taing.

Solveig left the house. She drifted down the long drive towards the gate. Beyond lay the fields and cliffs and the western sea.

Mrs Taing, busy at the baking board, could hear the low mingled murmurs from above, but not of course the actual words – though she did her best, dipping her ear, and tilting her head and shutting off the radio. The conversation went on for ten minutes or so, while Mrs Taing wiped her hands and began to spread an immaculate starched cloth on the table.

'HELL SINK YOU!' It was like a peal of thunder from above. It was succeeded by a series of mouse-like squeals and squeaks – then two soft thuds – then the rapid tattoo of an elderly lady's shoes down the wide oak stair – and finally the opening and crashing shut of the massive oak door. Through the kitchen window Mrs Taing observed Miss Claudia in full retreat down the drive. In half a minute she was lost to view behind the sycamore at the gate.

Mrs Taing found the captain trembling and exhausted in his rocking-chair.

'What's wrong now, man?' she said.

'That woman,' he breathed, 'and her birthday present. Look at it – those two abominations! I flung them at her. One hit her on her ugly greedy mouth!' ... On the carpet, three feet apart, lay a pair of new sealskin slippers.

'Pour me a cup of gin!' he roared.

'I won't,' said Mrs Taing firmly. 'You've had enough gin for one day.'

'I'll get it myself,' he said. 'Where's Solveig? Take the

slippers away and put them in the fire – into the red heart of it.'

Mrs Taing gathered the birthday present into her apron.

'One of my friends is dead because of that slut and her present,' said Captain Bressay.

When Solveig got back from the crags the sun was down. In the kitchen her mother had laid a plentiful table – cold ham and chicken, and bere bannocks and cheese, and apples and home-made gooseberry jam. The cake glimmered at anchor on the sideboard, with its freight of unlit candles.

'I've the turnips and tatties to see to yet,' she told Solveig. 'It'll be half an hour at least before we eat. You'd better go up and stir some sweetness into him. That Claudia was nearly his death an hour ago.'

Solveig found him in his rocking-chair, presiding over a conference of shadows. He seemed not to be aware of her, standing over by the door.

'I know,' he was saying, 'Shelmark's dead. They've made him into slippers and a couple of handbags. We all die. Some day soon I'll be meeting Shelmark in mid-Atlantic, off Rockall somewhere. Gather round, friends. Even a cave dies, after ten thousand years or so. Jenny dear, come and sit over here beside me where you always sit. Kind of you to come on my birthday ... You with the sheepskin on your shoulder, don't be frightened, you know me. Come and warm yourself at the fire ... The cave's destroyed, I heard the blasting, but they can't destroy the pictures in the cave – the treasures ... Well Pedro, old friend, it's good to see you again. How many harvests did you take in at Apgarth? – Never thought you'd come out of that cave alive, eh? ... Your majesty, King Robert, sit over there beside the stone-age boy – we're all equal here, no rank and grovelling, no nonsense like that ... Well Forg, well man, I'm sorry for you – could you not be content with the old boots and bottles you found in the ebb, man? That was a great fall you had. Never mind, Forg, you're welcome too ... If it isn't the laird himself, come back in rags from the cave to his old house – Jeremiah Alkirk, esquire! The Hall's come down in the world, eh – an old decrepit skipper sitting at your fire. What's that? – you don't mind – kindly spoken, sir ... Who's this? If it isn't that small boy Gib who was good to the tinkers one wild Christmas. Gib, I always like it when you come to see me. I would give you some chocolate but you're long past chocolate and lemon water and things like that ... Cheems, is that you? You never told me, Cheems, whether that sea-girl was at home the day you called with the ring, or not. We'll talk about it later, Cheems ... Who's that over there in the shadows? I know you, Eric Rolfson – the boy that found the pearl in the cave. It was the saving of Apgarth, that pearl. Go and speak to Jenny – wouldn't wonder if Jenny didn't leave the oyster there for you on purpose, Eric ... German lieutenant, come in. Don't hang back, man. There's no enemies here, now or ever. We're a band of brothers – the knights of the cave. I wish Solveig was here, so she could meet you all.'

There was silence for a short while. A first star shone through the tall window. Then the old man's voice fell once more on the shadows.

'The cave is dead. The treasures of the cave, gathered by you over a long long time – I've had the keeping of them since I was a boy. The ore they're finding in the crags is trash in comparison. Listen, friends, the pictures and images won't be lost. I'm handing them over to a new keeper – you know her – the girl Solveig who lives in this house – a very reliable good girl. Solveig will tell the stories to her children and her grandchildren. With luck, the stories will still be listened to, here in this island, in a hundred years' time.

When the stories are told no more, the island will be as lost as Atlantis.' ...

There were whispers and rustlings in the darkening room – but it might only have been the coal sinking in the grate, and the soft sift of ash. The skipper swung himself back and fore in his rocking-chair. He seemed to be in deep silent communion with the island immortals.

Suddenly Solveig was aware that his garnet eye was fixed on her. 'Have you been there all the time, girl?' he said. 'What do you mean by standing in the door and not speaking?'

'I thought you had company,' said Solveig.

'Company?' he said. 'What kind of company do I ever have? Look for yourself. There's nobody here.'

'Supper's ready,' cried Mrs Taing from the foot of the stair. 'Come and get it while it's hot.'

Solveig helped Sigurd out of his chair. The assembly of shadows was over. The living went slowly out of the room and down the wide curving stair, the old man with his withered hand on the girl's elbow.

When they stood at last in the kitchen door they saw on the sideboard the birthday cake. The candles were all lit now. It was a floating festival. It was like a great Viking funeral ship drifting into the sunset with its silver-heaped hero in the well.

The old man cried out with pleasure at the sight. But the sad thought came into Solveig's mind that this might well be the skipper's last birthday. He was much frailer now than he had been this day last year.

'A happy birthday,' said Mrs Taing to the old smiling sea-captain as he eased himself into the great oak chair of the Alkirks.